HORSE COUNTRY

Can't Be Tamed

Also by Yamile Saied Méndez

Blizzard Besties

Random Acts of Kittens

Wish Upon a Stray

Shaking Up the House

HORSE COUNTRY

BOOK 1
Can't Be Tamed

Yamile Saied Méndez

Scholastic Inc.

Copyright © 2022 by Yamile Saied Méndez
Interior art by Winona Nelson, © 2022 Scholastic Inc.

ISBN 978-1-338-74946-5

10 9 8 7 6 5 4 3 2   22 23 24 25 26

Printed in the U.S.A.   40
First printing 2022

Book design by Stephanie Yang

To Veeda Bybee, the best friend a person could have,

and to Patricia Méndez, a true Texan cowgirl

and the best mother-in-law.

1

Winds of Change

For some people, home smells like a fresh batch of chocolate chip cookies or like laundry softener. For Carolina Aguasvivas, home smelled like fresh hay and turned earth and that warm muskiness that only comes from a barn full of contented horses.

This early morning, on her way to the little barn to start the day's chores, the air also carried a hint of woodsmoke.

She did a double take when she realized the sign over the road that read *Orchard Farms* had been taken down. The poles and the frame stood like open arms waiting for the new sign. She wondered what name the new owner, Ms. Whitby, would choose for the property.

It had to be a special name because this was a special place.

Orchard Farms had been established just outside Paradise city limits almost two hundred years ago by old Mr. Bert Parry's great-grandparents. The Parrys were long gone. Carolina's dad, the ranch manager, kept everything running. The Aguasvivases lived in the caretaker cottage, which sat at the top of the hill next to an ancient apple orchard. Visitors to the ranch had to pass by her house first, which meant she always felt in the know. It was the only home she could remember, and she loved everything about it.

Her two-minute walk from home down to the ranch led her straight past the main house at the bottom of the hill. The mansion, as people called it, had been vacant for years. The town kids even said it was haunted. Mr. Parry hadn't visited the ranch in a long time, and he had finally sold it to Ms. Whitby.

The property was so large, Carolina couldn't see the whole thing from where she stood. Besides the cottage and the house, there were two barns, an indoor arena, three practice rings, and the pastures surrounding the property like a blanket.

The Idaho White Cloud Mountains ruled majestically in the background. This far into August, it was technically still summer, but the valley already glittered with frost.

The rumble of a white pickup truck's engine broke the sounds of songbirds as it passed her on the lane. A ribbon of steam rose from the exhaust when it stopped in the parking lot. Carolina stood on tiptoes to see if it was Ms. Whitby and her daughter. Excitement made her heart beat like a drum as her sturdy boots crunched on the gravel.

But at the sight of the two girls heading inside the big barn, her excitement fizzled out. Even from a distance, she recognized Loretta Sullivan and Tessa Wilson in their fancy matching riding outfits. The girls were in her grade—they were all starting sixth in a couple of weeks—but they weren't friends with her. Not anymore. Loretta glanced toward Carolina. She tossed her dark red ponytail over her shoulder and whispered something that made Tessa laugh.

Immediately, Carolina's defenses rose like a wall. She wished her best friend, Vida, were here with her. She missed her so much! Even if Vida didn't ride, she made things better when

Loretta and Tessa were around. A few more days, and Vida would be back from her family's yearly trip to the Philippines. Carolina couldn't wait. Especially if those two girls were going to be spending more time than usual at the ranch.

Winter season showing events were coming up. She had seen the signs pinned to the big barn bulletin board. Most likely Loretta and Tessa were here for lessons with their exclusive—and expensive—instructor. He came all the way from Boise. Those girls had never mucked a stall, and Carolina didn't care how great they looked riding; her dad had always said true horsemanship included all the horses' care.

And yet, jealousy prickled Carolina's heart. She didn't care about shows, but she too wanted to train with an instructor. A real-life one.

Carolina had the horse care part down: She mucked stalls, exercised the horses and fed them, and did any random jobs in exchange for riding time. Not with the fancy Boise instructor though. Not with the expensive show horses that boarded in the big barn, either. Even being the ranch manager's daughter couldn't give her that kind of benefit.

Horses cost a lot of money. And horse sports even more.

Between riding clothes, fees, the travel, the time away from the stables . . . It was a lot.

But riding the ponies or class horses that had remained after the riding clinic closed a couple of years ago was better than not riding at all. Which was the problem: The more time she spent with horses, the more obsessed she became.

One day when she had enough money, Carolina would ride whenever she wanted to. And not just any horse. No, it would be her heart horse, her forever friend. She would have a saddle with her initials and a proper riding outfit—

A horse neighed inside the little barn, bringing her back to the present. She smiled with anticipation, and jealousy tossed aside, she ran the last yards to her favorite place in the world.

The gate handle was cold as she pulled it down. The barn door slid open.

She took a deep breath and chanted, "Good morning, my loves!"

When the light switched on automatically, four heads poked over their stall doors.

"Nice to see you, Leilani, Bella, Pepino, and Twinkletoes!" she greeted them, walking along the main hallway of the barn.

The horses and the donkey nodded.

Horses come in a variety of breeds and sizes, and they're very different from donkeys. But they all have one thing in common: They just want affection. She patted them without hesitation. She loved the mossy softness of their noses, the coarse strength of their swishing tails, and the power they radiated—even Pepino, the gentlest horse that ever lived.

"Did you have a good night, Bella?" Carolina asked the painted miniature horse, who was the oldest and the smallest of the pack. She only reached up to Carolina's waist, but she had the biggest personality on the whole property.

Bella neighed regally, and behind her, Twinkletoes, the mini donkey, seemed to roll his eyes at the diva. Almost all horses needed their own space, but the two minis shared the biggest box stall. Twinkletoes was the same size as Bella, but a dusty gray color, with big friendly ears.

"How are you, Twinks?" she asked. "Did you have a good sleep?" She plucked sprigs of hay out of his tangled mane.

"After I clean your stall, I'll give you a good brush down so you can look your best for Ms. Whitby!"

Carolina's dad had wanted everything to look *immaculate* for her arrival.

Carolina had scrubbed the stalls the night before, but work at the barn was never-ending. It was the same routine day in, day out. She wouldn't have it any other way.

"Meow," a scratchy voice greeted her from the rafters.

"Oh, Your Majesty!" Carolina said, dipping into a curtsy. "I'm sorry, I hadn't seen you."

Luna, the tabby barn cat, blinked at her, then turned her gaze toward the entrance. She darted to hide behind the bales of hay stacked all the way to the ceiling.

Carolina heard footsteps.

"Oh, it's you! My favorite daughter!" Papi said. "I thought Bella had decided to finally start speaking her mind and boss us all around."

Carolina laughed. She ran back to the entrance to hug him.

Her dad put down the two pails he was carrying and hugged her back. "Hmmm, your hair smells of sunshine already!"

"You, on the other hand, smell like . . ." She sniffed his denim jacket. "Woodsmoke? What were you doing?"

"Earlier this morning we made a bonfire to send Tyler off." There was a mixture of sadness and pride in his voice.

A couple of years ago, Tyler had been one of the town's troublemakers. But Papi believed in second chances, so he took the boy under his wing. He'd gone through a similar thing when he was young. It had only taken one person to teach him a different way of doing things. Things he learned working at a barn after he met his heart horse, Capitán.

Working with horses became more than a job for him. It was a vocation. He'd once told Carolina that Capitán had saved his life. And Carolina realized that working with horses had saved Tyler's too.

Now he was leaving for college.

"We're all going to miss him," Carolina said.

Bella snorted. Tyler had been her favorite person.

Papi smiled and nodded. "Yes, but I'm happy for him too." He put his index finger up. "And for us. We're going to have a lot of fun this year with all the changes coming. Just you wait."

Papi took off his San Diego Padres baseball cap. Once upon a time, the hat had been blue. Now after all these years, the sun had bleached it to a light gray. Papi's dark brown curly hair was the same shade and texture as Carolina's. Hers fell all the way to her waist. His was short and had a few silver touches at the temples.

As the sun had bleached the hat, it had tanned his skin to dark brown. He spent all his days—and many nights—outdoors, at work.

"Fun?" she asked, faking shock. "You mean it's not all work work work?"

"Winds of change are blowing. Can't you feel them?" He threw his head back, eyes closed as if he could really feel a magical breeze. His mustache twitched as he smiled.

"Did the wind blow away the old sign too?"

He laughed. "Once Ms. Whitby approved the new name, the sign went straight into the bonfire."

Papi had never complained that Mr. Parry was such a distant boss, but now he seemed absolutely giddy that the new one was much more involved.

"What's the new name?" Carolina asked, pulling on his sleeve.

He mimicked zipping his lips. "Patience!" he said, and ruffled her hair.

"I can't wait!" she exclaimed. His excitement was contagious.

"Nothing better to speed the clock than getting to work, then," he said, clapping his hands once. "Remember, Twinkletoes is still on a special diet. He and Bella should eat from these pails. Okay?" He rolled up his sleeves, revealing the fading blue tattoo of a cross on his forearm. Then he picked up the pails and moved them next to the stall the mini donkey and the miniature mare shared.

Carolina had done these chores before, but still, she took mental note of all his instructions.

"I see you have things under control, but if you need anything at all, call me. Or you can ask any of the guys. There are some new faces joining us, but the main core will remain the same."

She narrowed her eyes at him. "What do you mean? New workers? Tyler is the only person leaving." She knew there was a new owner, but not about anybody else. Surely they couldn't be trying to replace her family?

Papi smiled, and wrinkles fanned out from the corners of his eyes. "Don't worry, mi amor—everyone else is staying. But there might just be a few new instructors—including a new trainer. She's excited to start teaching as soon as possible."

A woman horse trainer! Carolina had never been able to work with one before.

Carolina was so excited she jumped and clapped. Pepino tossed his head up as if to say, "What's the big news?"

Her heart galloped fast and furiously as she drew a deep breath and asked, "So . . . can I still ride after my work is done?"

"Yep," he said. "Thanks for asking for permission first."

A glow spread in her chest. She'd been working on not being so impulsive, and she was glad he'd noticed.

"Which horse can I take?"

Her dad scratched his head, making his hair point in every

direction. "Take Pepino. He needs the exercise. The older he gets, the lazier he becomes. Remember, stay in the small arena. I'd rather you didn't ride alone on the trails today."

She sighed but didn't complain. Pepino was the mellowest pony on the planet. She gave his white muzzle a scratch. Papi had named him Pepino because when he first arrived, he'd acted cool as a cucumber around the rest of the herd. The name in Spanish had stuck. As for riding in the arena, she had expected it. At least from there she could see when the owners arrived.

Once again, she hugged her dad. "Thank you, Papi. I promise to obey you in everything and make you proud."

She looked up at him in time to see sparkles in his eyes. "You already make me proud." He kissed her forehead. "Oh, and before I forget, wear a helmet, please."

"Whatever you say, boss," she said.

Papi winked at her and left. She stood watching his backlit outline as he returned to the big stable, and wished for the courage to ask if she could ride one of the show horses instead.

They needed exercise too, and in most cases, their owners needed help from the stable hands.

But before she could form the words to ask, Papi was already gone.

Luna the cat meowed from the rafters.

"I know, Luna," Carolina said, sticking her tongue out at her. "I'm going."

The best motivation in the world is getting to ride when you're done. So Carolina got right to work, wondering when she'd get her first glimpse of the owner and her daughter.

2

First Impressions

By the time she was done with the last and messiest stall, the one that housed Twinkletoes and Bella, Carolina had worked up a sweat. She'd taken off her hoodie, tied back her hair, and tripped on Luna once or twice.

The cat kept trying to check that she had done a good job. Finally satisfied, Luna climbed to the top of the bales of hay. Wrapped in a tight ball, she went to sleep without even one meow of complaint.

Carolina's cheeks were flushed. Her arms ached. But the scent of eucalyptus and lemon spread through the stable from washing the floors. Everything was sparkling—or at least, as clean as a horse barn could ever get.

Hopefully Ms. Whitby would arrive before the horses had a chance to make their mess all over again. Since it was sunny, they could stay in the pasture until the evening. But if the weather report was accurate and another storm blew in, tomorrow would be an indoor day. Then Carolina would have to pick up manure and set clean bedding in the evening as well as in the morning.

She made sure she had swept every corner, and once she confirmed everything was spotless, she dashed to the pasture to fetch Pepino, lead rein in hand and horse treats in her pocket.

It was finally time to ride.

· U ·

"I love you too, Twinkletoes." Carolina gently shoved him back. The donkey was clinging to her, trying to wrap himself around her. "Come on, Pepino!"

Pepino, a sorrel with a flaxen mane and tail, was too busy chewing the sweet grass along the fence. Carolina wasn't above begging or bribing though. She showed him the snack she had in a little bucket, and with it lured him toward the gate. Then he lowered his head to claim his prize.

She clipped the lead rope to his green halter.

Gently, she coaxed the pony out of the pasture, and he followed her to the grooming stall, where she would get him clean and put on his gear, or tack. The heavy felt pad and the saddle that fit Pepino waited on the portable saddle stand.

Carolina started brushing him carefully and he stood still. Pepino knew all the steps of this pre-ride ritual. He closed his eyes, contented as she untangled his mane and used each brush in the right order. Dust rose in plumes that made her sneeze, and she placed a calming hand on his side, just in case she'd startled him. At her touch, he exhaled deeply.

Once she had carefully cleaned out his hooves with a pick, she tacked him up. Carefully she carried out each of the steps to putting on his saddle. Her dad had shown her how since she was a little girl. Finally, once she had gotten the bridle onto his head and the bit into his mouth, she grabbed her helmet and Pepino's reins.

"All done," she said. "Let's go, Pep."

She could hardly contain her enthusiasm as they marched to the small arena.

Two of the stable hands—Juan Carlos, who everyone called JC, and Andrew—were admiring the new sign they'd installed next to the entrance of the big barn.

Welcome to Paradise Ranch.

"Paradise Ranch?" she called out.

They turned around, smiling.

JC tipped his cowboy hat at her in greeting.

"Do you like the new name?" Andrew asked, his bright blue eyes glittering with pride.

"It's perfect," she replied.

She really did love it.

Their ranch was truly paradise. It seemed she and Ms. Whitby were on the same wavelength. She was feeling impatient to meet her.

Sensing she was distracted, Pepino stopped by one of the practice barrels, probably to check if it had any salt.

Gently, she pulled on his reins, resuming her walk to the arena.

"Speaking of signs, no sign of Ms. Whitby yet?" she asked.

"Not yet," JC replied. "Won't be long though. See you later, *Carolina.*"

She laughed at the way he mispronounced her name, *Caro-lie-na,* like the state. Ever since she was little, she'd insisted people pronounce it *Caro-lee-na*, like in Spanish. Everyone complied except for JC, who liked to tease her about it still.

"See you later, *Juan Carlos!*" she teased him back.

He wrinkled his nose at her, and they all laughed.

The men waved as they headed toward the main office, and she waved back.

She opened the gate to the fenced outdoor arena, which had comfy footing for the horses and plenty of space for them to work. Once Pepino walked in, Carolina promptly closed the gate behind her. Horses were escape masters. She didn't want to be chasing Pepino when the new owner arrived.

Carolina tied up his reins so they wouldn't trip him up and clipped a long, long lead line to his bridle so they could start with groundwork. Dutiful Pepino immediately began his wide, slow circle around Carolina, with the line connecting them together and Carolina's hands directing his speed and direction.

From the corner of her eye, she saw Loretta and Tessa

watching her from the parking lot. She felt proud of how well she was working with Pepino, and all by herself to boot.

Carolina knew right when he was happy and warmed up enough: His ear turned toward her as he cantered. He licked his lips and chewed on the bit in his mouth. He lowered his head, and his circle shrank, smaller and smaller, until he slowed to a jog, then a walk. He finally stopped and sighed loudly.

Pepino was ready for the join-up, that moment when the horse is ready for its rider. He knew she was in charge. Carolina stood at an angle, not looking in his eye. She calmed her breath until he walked in her direction meekly.

He wrapped his head around her in a hug.

She patted him lovingly. His back was warm. They'd both worked up a sweat.

"You're such a good, good horse." She kissed his soft nose.

Finally, she retightened the cinch of the saddle, which secured it snugly around his belly, and snapped her helmet on. She then led him to the mounting block. She hopped on his back and made sure the stirrups were the perfect length for her legs.

"And . . . walk," she commanded.

Recognizing the authority in her voice, the pony walked resolutely around the ring, and when she pressed him with her left leg, he obediently changed direction away from it. She lifted her gaze and saw Andrew, JC, and Papi watching her from the main office. Pepino slowed down.

"Trot," she said, gently tightening her legs around his belly, to remind him who the leader was—and to prove to her audience that she could take charge.

The pony picked up his pace.

Carolina instinctively started posting, rising up and down along with Pep's rhythmic two-step gait. Without waiting for a verbal command, and maybe because he felt she was perfectly balanced, he switched into a lope.

The rhythm changed, and she fought against her initial impulse to raise her knees. Instead, she controlled her breathing and pushed her boots down in the stirrups. She moved along with the horse as he increased his speed in a one-two-three rolling beat that felt like a merry-go-round. Just like Tyler had taught her.

Pepino wasn't a temperamental horse, but he could still cause trouble. Because he was so mellow, he could be hard to lead. He always chose the path of least resistance, but like all horses, he also wanted to please his rider. And Carolina was becoming a great rider the more she practiced. He followed every one of her requests at the slightest twitch of the reins, crisscrossing the arena in figure eights and full circles. Finally, Carolina had forgotten about everyone watching her enough to truly connect with Pepino. It was as if the pony could guess her thoughts.

And when Pepino noticed a black SUV had parked next to the main office, so did Carolina.

To her surprise, her audience had grown.

Leaning against the white wooden fence of the circular arena, a girl Carolina had never seen before watched her intensely. She wore a brown suede jacket with fringe and beautiful embroidered green boots. Next to her stood a woman.

The girl's skin and hair were as dark as Carolina's, but the woman, who could be none other than Ms. Whitby, the new stable owner, was pale and had dark blond hair. She wore just plain jeans and a black jacket, and she looked at the surroundings with pride and love, like she owned everything in sight. Which she did.

Carolina hadn't heard the new owners' arrival!

She smiled at them as the surprise switched to delight. The girl must be Ms. Whitby's daughter. In these parts of Idaho, Carolina didn't usually meet a lot of people who looked like her.

She led Pepino to the side of the fence and pulled him into a halt.

"Hello," she said, her heart slowly returning to a resting pace after the adrenaline and exercise of riding.

Carolina noticed mother and daughter had the same piercing hazel eyes. Their features were similar, elegant and sharp at the same time. But their expressions couldn't have been more different. The girl looked serious and guarded. But the woman smiled radiantly.

"You must be Amado and Jen's daughter, Carolina."

"I am." Carolina was happy that Ms. Whitby knew her name—and how to pronounce it.

"You have excellent form! You sure made this pony work. Who taught you how to ride?"

Carolina felt herself blushing. "I took a few lessons here and there, but mostly I taught myself." Pepino snorted, interrupting Carolina before she started gushing about the Tina Hodges videos she watched obsessively on YouTube to learn new tricks. She gave him a pat. "Actually, the horses taught me too," she added.

Ms. Whitby laughed, but her daughter was looking toward the asphalt snake of the country road that led to the highway toward town.

"Maybe you could teach my daughter, Chelsie, a trick or two. Right, Chels?" said Ms. Whitby.

"Sure," the girl said in a quiet voice, but her attention was elsewhere. Was that why she hadn't at least said hello?

Carolina hoped so. She was about to ask Chelsie if she wanted to ride one of the barn horses when a navy-blue truck with a trailer came down the country road and pulled up next to the big barn.

Chelsie's face lit up with a smile. "She's here!" she said, and took off running toward the truck without a second glance at Carolina, who sighed, disappointed at the missed chance.

Ms. Whitby's friendly smile almost made up for her daughter's coldness. "It's nice to meet you." Then she added, "I hope you and Chelsie will become good friends."

Carolina nodded. "I'd love that," she said, trying to smile. But honestly? Chelsie's snub stung.

She'd been the only child at the ranch all her life. Her best friend, Vida, wasn't a horse person at all. Having a friend who loved horses as much as she did would be perfect. She'd heard Ms. Whitby had a daughter but hadn't known she'd be Carolina's age! She kept her eye on the girl—Chelsie—already imagining what she would show her first. If Chelsie gave her a chance.

While Carolina had Pepino take another round, she saw Papi and the other grooms greet the truck driver, a Black woman with a long braid down her back. She unlocked the big back door of the double trailer while Carolina's father and the other stable workers put down the ramp. A beautiful palomino mare gently backed down the ramp, and the woman handed the reins to JC. He led the horse to the big barn. Her cream-colored coat was shiny under the sun as she flicked her white tail.

Bored, Pepino started chewing the grass that grew among the pebbles on the edge of the arena, but Carolina was too distracted to stop him. The remaining horse in the trailer neighed nervously.

The woman tried to coax it out of the trailer, but it took a few tries until the beautiful horse dared to come out. It was a young mare.

The color of her sleek coat was a dark brown, or dark bay. Her black mane, tail, and legs made her a seal brown.

Carolina's mind flashed to the books she'd loved to read since she was a toddler. They had taught her horse colors as well as breeds.

This one seemed to be a Thoroughbred. Purasangre, in Spanish. Pure blood. Hot-blooded, spirited, agile, and wicked fast.

The mare was muscly like a sprinter. She must have been a racehorse before coming to Orchard Farms.

No. *Paradise Ranch*, Carolina corrected herself.

Andrew grabbed the horse's lead rope and encouraged the mare to walk off the ramp, but she tossed her mane and whinnied. The woman took the rope from him, and he stood admiring the newcomer with the rest of the people. Even from a distance, Carolina could tell there was a fire in the majestic animal. If it wasn't contained, it would burn not only her but everything around her, like the wildfires that threatened the mountains every year.

A minute ago, Chelsie had been excited by the arrival of the trailer. Now she stood behind her mom as the mare reared on her hind legs.

"Whoa," Carolina whispered, placing a hand over her heart.

The mare landed on her forelegs and snorted. But when she lifted her gaze, she seemed to be looking for something.

"Easy, girl," Carolina whispered again.

From across the distance, the Thoroughbred looked at her for a few seconds. She calmed down enough for the woman to get her bearings and coax her toward the big barn.

Pepino, unaware that anything had happened, chewed on the grass, and Carolina patted his mane softly. She loved the gentle pony, and he'd been a fun ride. But in that instant that she and the mare had locked eyes, a desire had been planted in her heart.

She should've pulled it before it took root, but she was in love.

Carolina wouldn't rest until she got to ride that beautiful mare.

3

The Thoroughbred

The rest of the day, the barn was a storm of change. Soon after the arrival of the new horses, a moving van pulled up to the big house and workers started unloading furniture. Carolina's mom was already by the mansion directing the movers inside.

Carolina saw Ms. Whitby head to the house in a trot, her arms pumping resolutely. Chelsie followed more slowly behind her, hands deep in her pockets, shoulders hunched and almost touching her ears.

Carolina's dad was welcoming a group of new stable hands.

She wondered if maybe she should offer to help. Maybe Chelsie would like a tour of the ranch this morning. But she had to put Pepino away and there were still a lot of chores to do at the small barn and no one else to do them. She was heading there when Andrew called her name and waved her over. He was next to a watering trough, talking with one of the newcomers, the woman who'd led the horses out of the trailer.

Carolina wanted to meet her and she led Pepino in their direction.

Andrew had lived in the area for much of his life and once upon a time had been a famous rodeo champion. He'd spent most of his sixty years on a horse, and when he was on his own two feet, he walked slightly bent and stiff legged.

"Hey, Andrew!" she said, and then looked at the woman. "Hi. I'm Carolina."

The woman smiled. "I'm Kimber. Nice to meet you."

"She's the new trainer," Andrew added with a glint in his eye. He knew how much Carolina wanted to learn from a proper instructor. His style was very different from what Carolina saw on YouTube videos. He too had mostly taught himself about horses.

But here was a real-life instructor. One who'd live at the ranch. Carolina's heart galloped in her chest like a wild pony.

"It's so great to have you here!" she said.

"I'm so excited to be here helping Ms. Whitby in this new chapter."

"You will have your job cut out for you," Andrew said. "It's starting almost from scratch, but there is a lot of need and demand for a new riding program in Paradise."

"That's what I heard," Kimber said. "I'm eager to set everything up, bring new horses, advertise for classes."

"Are the horses you brought part of the new riding program?" Carolina asked, her mind already thinking how fun it would be to ride the beautiful Thoroughbred. "Are they going to be showing or . . . something else?"

"The palomino's mine," Kimber said. "My parents gave her to me when I turned fifteen. Her name's Mercedes, but I call her Sadie."

"Fancy!" Carolina said.

Next to her, Pepino drank water like a camel, loudly and splashing everywhere. Carolina caught Andrew's eye; he shook his head and laughed.

"And the other one?" Carolina asked, her cheeks burning.

"The Thoroughbred is a real beauty, ain't she?" Andrew said. "I heard the new boss lady got her for her daughter."

"That's right," Kimber said.

"Lucky!" Carolina exclaimed before she could stop herself. How she wished she could have a horse of her own. A horse of her heart, like Sadie was Kimber's. Like her dad had Capitán when he was a young boy. Even old Mr. Parry had a horse he'd loved above all others. Andromeda. There was even a stained-glass window in the big barn he'd had done specially to remember the black horse he'd loved as a kid.

She imagined herself bonding with that beautiful mare, riding together on the trails. She was lost in her thoughts until Andrew's words snagged her attention.

"That is, if she can acclimate to her new home," Andrew said. "She's spirited. Might not work well for the young girl."

"Why wouldn't she?" Carolina asked. "Acclimate here, I mean." She couldn't imagine the horse not fitting in.

Andrew grimaced. "She's a young horse, only about five, but she's made the rounds already, right?"

"Yep," Kimber confirmed.

"What do you mean?" Carolina asked.

"She was on the Road to the Kentucky Oaks but didn't make the cut. Ever since, she's been moved from stable to stable, poor thing," Kimber said.

The world of horse racing was unfamiliar to Carolina. The ranch boarded show horses. Carolina had never competed in a show, but she had seen plenty of them from when the ranch hosted them. Races were a whole other thing though. She'd never even watched one on TV, much less attended one. But of course she'd heard about the Kentucky Derby and the other two events that were part of the Triple Crown—the Preakness Stakes and the Belmont Stakes.

She scratched her head. "The Kentucky Derby?"

Andrew shook his head. "Not the Derby. The Oaks. It's just for three-year-old Thoroughbred fillies. But the road to it is a grueling business. It breaks some animals. And then they get tossed aside like discarded toys."

Carolina shivered. Pepino stepped closer to her as if he wanted to reassure her that at Paradise Ranch, no one—horse or human—was tossed away.

"Is that what happened to her?" she asked.

Kimber nodded. "She couldn't handle the pressure." Then she shrugged. "Or maybe it was her rider. Who knows?"

"What's her name?" Carolina asked, her desire to meet the mare stronger than ever.

"Velvet," Kimber said. "Her full name is Midnight Velvet."

Carolina could imagine the softness of the mare's nose on her fingertips. The name was perfect.

Kimber sighed. "I better get back to her. The long ride from California and the last few months have taken a toll on the poor creature. Once Dr. Rooney takes a look at her, we can start planning her rehabilitation."

Dr. Rooney was the vet who took care of every animal that lived on the ranch. He was a miracle worker. Velvet had come to the right place.

"That's a nasty wound on her leg," Andrew said. "What happened?"

Kimber clicked her tongue and pressed her lips. "It's a bed sore that wasn't treated properly," she sighed. "Chelsie is sup-posed to start showing with her in the spring, but if she's not ready by sign-ups, I don't want to take the risk. So we'll see in the next few weeks or so."

Andrew whistled. "That's right. Sign-ups for spring close in early September."

Early September was only three weeks away.

"That's not a lot of time," Carolina said, picturing the calendar on the bulletin board, September seventh circled in glowing red.

She wondered what would happen to Velvet if she didn't heal in time. She wanted to go see her. Meet her properly. Maybe there was something she could do to help speed up the process. She had experience helping animals heal. Like Twinkletoes. She was excited just thinking about asking Kimber if she could take a look.

But she didn't get to ask because right that second, her dad showed up.

"You need to eat lunch, Caro," her dad said, and her bubble of excitement popped. "Mom left you a cooler in the small barn. Go and eat, and then finish your chores. What else are you missing?"

"Leilani is waiting for her turn," she said.

"Do you need help?" Papi asked.

She shook her head. She wanted to show her dad, Andrew, Kimber, and all the newcomers that she could handle the small responsibilities she had. Maybe they'd see she was ready for more. "I got it. Thanks though. Come on, Pepino."

Pepino clip-clopped obediently behind her. This, she could handle.

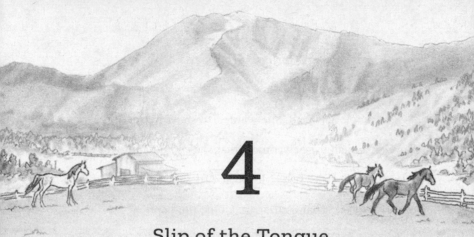

4

Slip of the Tongue

When Pepino was ready to join his herd in the pasture, Leilani neighed with happiness that her friend was back. She trotted to meet Pepino as if eager to hear his news.

Now that the sun had come out, the temperature had spiked. Carolina was sweaty, dusty, and tired but satisfied with her work. She went back to the coolness of the barn to eat her lunch.

Her mom had sent down a sandwich for her—homemade flatbread, carne asada, caramelized onions, and avocado. One of Abuela Cecilia's specialties. Mom had mastered it although she didn't have a drop of Latina in her.

Carolina's heritage was a mix: Irish on the Murphy side

(her mom's) and Mexican Argentine on the Aguasvivas one (her dad's). Besides being a wonderful cook, her dad's mom, Abuela Cecilia, was famous for her soft voice and firm touch that could soothe the fussiest baby or the most spirited stallion. Carolina's dad often said she'd inherited the gift to charm horses from her abuela. Connecting with them came naturally to her.

Now, what if she could use her gifts to help Velvet? But how? While she ate, she thought of ways to get close to the mare.

In that moment, Luna slunk inside the barn and rubbed her arched back against Carolina's leg.

"Meow."

Carolina caught a glance at the clock, and her heart flip-flopped. There were so many things to do before the sun set.

She felt overwhelmed with all the work for a second, but she remembered how much she'd insisted on doing things herself instead of asking JC or Andrew for help.

There was no time to despair.

Ms. Whitby was bound to go on a tour of the small barn,

and Carolina wanted everyone, including Twinkletoes, to look their best. She went out and brought him to the barn for his beautifying session.

Grooming Twinkletoes required some extra care. The process wasn't the same as grooming a horse. It was impossible to get him perfectly clean because he was always rolling in the grass and dirt. Besides, his winter coat was already growing in. Tyler had once told Carolina that donkeys have air pockets in their coat for insulation against the cold, and that it was important not to destroy them with excessive brushing.

She put on music, some of her dad's favorite '90s beats, secured Twinkles in the aisle, and set to work. Twinkletoes might as well have been at a spa judging by the contented expression on his face. When she was done braiding his mane, she heard voices getting closer—a woman's voice and her dad saying, "Caro is very dependable and responsible for her age."

Ms. Whitby was here!

Carolina rushed to finish making Twinkletoes look presentable.

"Hi," a pleasant voice said behind her.

She turned around and came face-to-face with Ms. Whitby. Chelsie hung out a few steps behind her mom, as if she were scared of something. It couldn't be anything in the barn now, could it?

Chelsie had her nose turned up as if the smell offended her. Carolina's heart prickled. She'd been proud of how clean everything looked. She wondered what she could do to befriend the girl. She hadn't seemed particularly friendly earlier. But then, she'd been distracted with Velvet's arrival.

Living on the same property and with her family's livelihood depending on the Whitbys, Carolina figured she was bound to become friends with Chelsie, right? They might even have a lot more in common than a love for horses, though Carolina would never know if she didn't talk to her.

Papi was looking around the barn, and he nodded as if he approved of her work—and the music, although it was a little too loud for polite conversation. With a smile back on her face, Carolina turned the music down just a notch.

"Hi, Ms. Whitby. Hi, Chelsie," Carolina said carefully. "Nice to meet you properly."

"Nice to meet you, Carolina," Ms. Whitby said, stretching out her hand to shake. "Call me Heather."

Carolina realized her hand was covered in donkey hair, and instead offered her elbow for a bump instead.

They both laughed. But Chelsie smirked, and Carolina wondered if that had been a dorky thing to do.

Twinkletoes snorted and shook his mane. He'd learned a few things from Bella, the attention seeker. But at least he'd broken through the brief awkwardness.

"Oh, who is this handsome boy here?" Ms. Whitby— Heather—said, patting the donkey's back.

"This is Twinkletoes, Twinks or Twinkles for short," Papi said. "Named after the main character of a favorite TV show my daughter got me hooked on."

"I think I know which one you're talking about. Now tell me, what's the story behind this mini donkey?" she asked.

Papi and Carolina exchanged a charged look.

Twinkletoes's story wasn't a pretty one, although it had a happy ending. Or a happy present.

"Do you want to tell it?" Papi asked, and he leaned against

one of the walls. He'd never admit it, but he was tired. And the workday wasn't close to being done.

Carolina nodded, pausing for a second to decide where to start. She didn't know why, but she felt like she had to make sure Heather knew how much the donkey meant to all of them. She was bound to be taking stock of everything at the ranch, and Carolina couldn't imagine Twinkletoes not being part of it. She felt the urge to make a good case for him.

Finally, she took a deep breath and said, "One Sunday afternoon, we were driving around town, and in a spur-of-the-moment decision, Papi turned in to a neighborhood we'd never been through before. Most of the new houses had large yards. Some had horses and goats fenced in. But there was one that had a brand-new trampoline—with an animal tied to it."

She noticed this got Chelsie's attention, although the girl wasn't looking at her. Instead, she kept her gaze on Luna, who was up on her rafter.

"I actually thought it was a big dog," Papi said, his eyebrows twitching in perfect synchronicity with Luna's swishing tail.

"Twinkletoes was tied up to a trampoline?" Heather's

expression was a mixture of horror at the situation, pity for the donkey, and anger at the people who had put him there. Some people who dealt with expensive race and show horses didn't pay attention to ponies or donkeys, as if they were lesser creatures. It seemed Heather was not like *some people,* and Carolina liked her more and more by the second.

Carolina continued, "I made Papi stop the car, and Twinkletoes looked at us and huffed."

"As if he'd been waiting for us and wondered what had taken so long," Papi added, scratching Twinkle's mane. "A man came out of the house and asked if we were interested in taking the donkey off his hands." Papi took over the thread of the story like an expert weaver. "He said his daughter wanted a mini donkey because they're so cute and they heard they make good guard animals, but they realized they didn't know how to take care of him. Poor Twinkles even had a wound on his leg from being tied so long. Everyone was miserable."

He left out the part about the flies that had swarmed around the donkey, and the way he flinched when the man raised his voice, as if wary of making a wrong move.

"Luckily, we had the trailer with us. We were gone before the man changed his mind," Carolina said. "And Twinkles has been with us ever since."

Twinkletoes swished his tail although there were no flies to shoo away.

"You all have done an amazing job taking care of him," Heather said.

"It's mostly been Caro," Papi said, and Carolina's chest about burst with pride. She kept her gaze down.

But then Chelsie said, "I heard that donkeys do better in pairs though. Is he the only donkey here? I mean . . . is that okay for him to be the only one?"

Why would Chelsie even ask this? Carolina's smile dropped. Now was not the time to bring this up. What if Heather was still deciding on which animals to keep? What if she decided to re-home him?

"He and Bella are friends," Carolina replied, avoiding Chelsie's eyes in case the other girl saw how her careless comment had affected her.

Twinkles, a sponge for feelings, lowered his head, as if he

knew they were talking about his future and felt sorry for himself.

"Aw! Look at his face!" Heather exclaimed, and kissed the donkey's forehead. "I'm sure he's everyone's favorite here."

"He is," Papi said.

Carolina noticed how Chelsie had raised her eyebrows as if she weren't convinced Twinkletoes belonged here. What did she know about how happy the donkey was? A protective wall rose in Carolina's heart as a result.

The adults didn't seem to notice the air was tense again. Heather and Papi talked about how Carolina had treated the wound on Twinkle's leg.

"We can try that with Velvet," Carolina said when Heather crouched to take a better look at the healed scar. Once, it had been raw and painful. Now it was a silver line that looked like an anklet.

When Heather stood up again, she smiled at Carolina. "His toes are so clean, they do seem to twinkle. Good job, Carolina."

Once again, her chest glowed with pride for a job well done.

"I hope Velvet likes it here. Let's hope she adapts . . ." Carolina said, repeating Kimber's words from earlier.

"I hope so too," Papi said.

Heather had a skeptical expression on her face. "We'll have to see. Like Twinkles's previous home, sometimes people have the best intentions and then reality shows them the truth. Sometimes even a good place still isn't a good match for the animals, and they have to move on."

"Not Velvet, Mom," Chelsie said. Her voice was alarmed, and she sent Carolina a pointed look.

Carolina hadn't meant anything about Velvet adapting. She'd only repeated what she'd heard. How could Chelsie think she'd meant—

"Velvet needs to learn how to trust humans again. Maybe we should've leased instead of buying her so impulsively." Heather sighed, as if she had a huge weight in her heart.

Carolina met Chelsie's eyes. The new girl looked as dismayed as Carolina felt. And as defensive.

"Time will tell. And now, let's go, Chels. We still need to unpack for tonight."

They said their good-nights and headed back to the mansion house.

Papi returned to the office for some paperwork.

Carolina watched them all go, feeling like she shouldn't have said so much, but at the same time that she should've explained more. She should've made sure they understood they were all on the same page. Chelsie had taken her words the opposite way Carolina had meant them! It was like Ms. Whitby's daughter was determined to remain as distant as possible from her.

She wished she could talk back through the whole conversation with Vida, who would know exactly how it went wrong. But her best friend was still in the Philippines on her annual summer trip to visit her family.

Carolina had to finish her chores if she wanted to visit Velvet. Quickly, she brought the horses back to their stalls for the night. All the while, she was trying to figure out how to make sure the mare felt right at home, just like Twinkletoes did. If she didn't heal in three weeks, she couldn't be signed up to show in the spring. And if she couldn't show in the spring . . . It sounded like Heather already had doubts about Velvet. Would Heather give up on the spirited, troubled mare?

Since she'd put her foot in her mouth, Carolina was determined to help. She had to save Velvet and show everyone that she belonged here.

5

It's Not Fair

"How did it go?" Mom asked at the dinner table.

Papi had eaten and gone straight to bed. He'd been working nonstop since before dawn, and who knew when he'd have a day off. Carolina and Mom still sat at the little wooden table in the corner of the kitchen.

"I like Kimber, the new trainer, and Ms. Whitby. I didn't get to talk to her a lot, but she was nice. She said I could call her Heather. How was your day?" Carolina asked. She scooped a last, cheesy bite of Mom's enchiladas into her mouth. She'd been starving by the time she came home.

"This afternoon I helped Heather put some of her books away

on the office bookshelves. She has an impressive collection." Her mom undid the practical bun on top of her head, and her auburn hair cascaded in soft curls onto her shoulders. She practically wore the same thing Carolina had on, a flannel shirt and jeans, but she always looked put together. Carolina wondered how she did it.

"You really like her, don't you?"

Mom had been a teacher years ago. The way to her heart was paved in books.

"I actually like her a lot. She has all these dreams for the ranch!" Mom said. "I can tell the whole town will be re-invigorated with the Whitbys' arrival. Not just the ranch. There will be so many new job openings now that we'll be a fully functional property again."

Carolina listened to her in silence, loving the pictures her mom's enthusiasm painted in her mind.

Mom placed a second serving on Carolina's plate and added, "Chelsie's very nice too."

Carolina shrugged. "You think?" She tried not to make a face, but she had clearly failed.

Mom placed her fist on her hip and shook her head. "Trouble in paradise? Already?"

Carolina chewed slowly to gain some time before she replied, "She seems . . . kind of stuck up. Like the typical horse girls from all those old TV shows you love to watch."

Mom laughed, pretending to be offended. But maybe it wasn't all pretending, because she said, "Caro . . ." There was a warning in her voice. "How could you know that already?"

How could she explain how cold Chelsie had acted toward her? How could she say it was a gut feeling without sounding envious of Chelsie's nice clothes, or like she was reading too much into the misunderstanding during their conversation at the little barn? Chelsie had ignored her immediately when she and her mom showed up. She'd made a mean comment about Twinkletoes and then acted as if Carolina had meant that this place wasn't a good match for Velvet. It was day one, but Carolina felt like they had no hope of becoming friends.

Then again, maybe her mom was right. Carolina knew that sometimes she was impulsive. It was probably unfair to judge Chelsie on a few exchanged words.

Carolina wiped her mouth with her cloth napkin as if she could wipe her words away too. "I guess I'll give her another chance."

"I guess you will," Mom said. "Please try to help her feel welcome. This is a big move for Chelsie, coming from California and all. You don't remember, but those first months here at the ranch were hard for you."

"But, Mom, how can you compare? I was a baby and I missed Grandma Ceci!" Carolina said, hating how whiny her voice sounded. But she couldn't help it. "How hard can her life be with all she has? I'd do anything to have a horse like Velvet."

Instead of telling her off, Mom brushed a hand over Carolina's head and gazed at her with so much love and patience. "Since when do the things we own make us happy? Remember, it's our relationships with people—and animals— that make a difference in our lives."

Mom was in one of her teaching moods, and Carolina resisted the urge to roll her eyes—even though Mom was right.

Partly.

Carolina didn't own a horse, but still, some of the happiest moments of her life had been shared with the lesson horses that belonged to Mr. Parry, and now Heather.

She was lucky her parents' work gave her access to them. But what would she have done if she had to depend on leasing a horse and her family couldn't afford it? And all these changes people kept talking about sounded great, but Carolina had a feeling it would be the same people from the community who'd benefit from them. While her barn family did all the work.

"It's not fair," Carolina muttered, eyeing her mom for a reaction.

Her mom sighed and took one of Carolina's hands and pressed it. "Pretend you're the new ranch owner. What would you do differently from Mr. Parry if you had a chance?"

The question was so unexpected, at first, she didn't know what to say. "Here at the ranch?"

Mom nodded. She didn't work outdoors much, but this summer had left a trail of new freckles on the creamy skin of her face. Her eyes were bright blue, like flakes of a cloudless sky.

"I . . ." Carolina hesitated. All of a sudden, she felt shy. Would

Mom understand? Carolina took a deep breath and continued, "A little bird told me there might be a new horse-riding lesson program."

"Oh, what else did that little bird say?" Mom asked in a playful voice.

Carolina smiled, but her mind was whirling with ideas that had been lurking under the surface for just the right time.

"Lessons can be so expensive, you know?"

Mom nodded, her lips pressed. She kept the barn's accounting books, so she knew what Carolina was talking about.

"I've been thinking about how Tyler sometimes taught me lessons in exchange for all the work I put in at the little barn. Do you think . . ." She took a deep breath and said, "Do you think Kimber could teach me? I know lessons are expensive. But if I save from birthdays and Christmas, plus working, then . . . what do you think?"

Mom's eyes were bright. "I love that idea. In fact, Heather told me that Chelsie will also have to work for lessons."

"Work where?" Carolina asked. There was a lot of work on the property, but the little barn was hers.

Oh, is it? a mean little voice in her mind asked.

Of course the little barn wasn't hers or her family's. Just like nothing on the property was. They just worked here. But would Chelsie take this from her too?

"Chelsie was telling her mom about a read-to-a-horse program she heard about on the radio. Maybe she'll read to the horses in the big barn," Mom said.

As long as it was in the big barn, Carolina didn't care.

"That's not really work though, is it?" she said, shrugging a shoulder like it wasn't a big deal, although if she was honest, it sounded cool. "It's like the program the pet shelter has in Boise for dogs and cats."

Mom laughed at her attitude and Carolina smiled in spite of herself.

"I think you two have a lot more in common than you think," Mom said. "Did you know her dad is from Argentina?"

Carolina was surprised. "Like Grandma Ceci?"

"Yes, like your grandma Ceci. Chelsie's dad moved back to Buenos Aires a few months ago. That's close to Entre Ríos, where your grandma's family is from."

That explained why Heather and Chelsie didn't look alike. Perhaps like Carolina, Chelsie took after her dad's side of the family instead of her mom's.

She was considering all this new information in silence when the clock on the wall struck the top of the hour.

Just on cue, a yawn caught Carolina off guard.

"What a day!" she said, stretching her arms as high as they could reach.

"Time for bed, cowgirl." Mom stood up and kissed her head before picking her laptop back up. "Tomorrow will be another long day and there's rain in the forecast."

Carolina loved the rain, but wet weather made things so much messier.

As she helped clean up after dinner, she went over all the things she'd need to do tomorrow: put down extra bedding for the horses, prepare more water stations that wouldn't freeze, give the leather tack a little extra TLC, and maybe even teach one of the horses how to jump over puddles. Pepino wouldn't cooperate, but maybe Leilani would be up to it? But only if all the chores got done.

In other circumstances, she would've thought how nice it would be to have extra hands at the barn. But not if Chelsie was taking work from her. She needed to earn lesson time.

"Good night, Mom," she said with a kiss.

Once in her room, she looked out her window at the best view of the newly renamed Paradise Ranch: The sky had turned a deep dark velvet and the stars glittered like ice.

The trees swayed with the breeze that was supposed to bring rain during the night. Papi had talked about winds of change. And there had been so many changes already. A new name for the ranch. A more involved owner. A full-time trainer. Maybe—hopefully?—a new friend in Chelsie. And Velvet.

Suddenly, a horse neighed in the big stable. The sound tugged at Carolina's heart like a lead rope, and she rushed back to the window to peer into the darkness.

6

Velvet at Midnight

In the mansion down the hill, a light on the top floor had come on. There was the outline of a person standing by the other window, but before Carolina could figure out if it was Chelsie, the light went off.

The horse called anxiously again from the big barn. Where Velvet was spending her first night.

Alone. Afraid. Confused.

Carolina's first impulse was to run and comfort a creature that was suffering. But before she rushed to its side, she remembered she wasn't supposed to go in the big barn unsupervised. Especially not on the night the new owner had arrived.

But what if no one else knew how to comfort Velvet?

She debated for a few minutes. After the long day of work, everyone was exhausted. For a few hours, no one would walk the property to check that things were okay. That had been Tyler's job.

There were no cameras to worry about either. Mr. Parry hadn't invested much in modernizing the barn.

Maybe those changes would come later, but for now, who would see her if she snuck in for a quick visit?

This morning, she'd promised her dad to be obedient. But Velvet was alone on her first night at Paradise and she was crying. Carolina wasn't sure what she would say if anyone caught her. What if Chelsie came over from the mansion? Would she be mean or tattle on her?

Carolina decided she couldn't be scared of the other girl. She wouldn't be able to sleep if she didn't at least make sure the mare was okay.

Carolina waited until she heard her mom close the door to their bedroom, pulled her jacket on, carefully stepped down the stairs, and made her way to the back door, where her boots were waiting.

The stars pulsed brightly as if aware they had only a couple of hours at most before the storm blew in and erased them. Carolina saw her breath rise in wisps toward the sky.

Every few seconds, she heard soft neighing and her heart clutched inside her with pity for Velvet.

She ran, pulled down the hill by the thought of seeing the mare.

The dew had frozen into frost and it crunched under her boots. A coyote howled somewhere in the mountains. Or at least she hoped it was a coyote, which would be a bit less scary than if it was a wolf from the newly reestablished packs in the area.

She'd have to make sure to close everything tightly so none of the animals got into trouble. She'd be devastated if anything happened to any of them because she'd been careless.

The big barn loomed in front of her.

On her tiptoes, she lifted the latch of the entrance to the main stable and slid the giant door open just enough to slip inside. Immediately, the scent of sleeping horses comforted her.

There was no one else around. Other than the sounds of

the night—the remaining crickets, horses snuffling in their stalls, and the blowing wind—there was soft silence broken by her echoing footsteps. Some of the horses peered at her curiously but went back to sleep. She wasn't their rider or their caretaker. They didn't give her a second glance.

The closer she walked to the last stall, the harder her heart beat.

A rustling sound startled her, and she halted. She peered into one of the stalls, but it was Kimber's palomino mare, Sadie. She opened one eye but soon closed it again, snoozing on her feet.

Carolina kept walking, looking for Velvet.

A horse pawed the ground. Its hooves click-clacked on the cement that was under the wood shavings. And if this was Velvet with her hurt leg, then she could injure herself even more.

Carolina ran the last few yards on her tiptoes and stood in front of the last stall.

At first, she couldn't see anything. But as her eyes adjusted, she realized that the mare was chewing on the wooden rail on the back of the stall.

Velvet made a grunting sound, and Carolina clicked her tongue to make her stop. Sometimes when horses were stressed, they got the bad habit of biting on a surface and sucking air. She remembered Dr. Rooney called this cribbing.

"Your tummy's going to hurt," she whispered.

There was a moment of silence.

Then Velvet nickered softly.

People smile. Horses nicker.

Velvet was smiling at her!

Carolina stepped closer to the stall's half door. She stood patiently. She didn't want to invade Velvet's space and make her nervous.

Until she heard Velvet stepping toward the door.

After a few endless seconds, the mare stood in front of Carolina. Under the feeble light that filtered in through the window, she saw Velvet's nostrils were round and relaxed, and so was her lower lip. Her tail flicked loosely, and her ears were pointing forward. All good signs. A small white star marked Velvet's forehead, slightly off center.

Finally, Velvet lowered her head close to Carolina's. The softness of Velvet's muzzle tickled her, but she couldn't help nuzzling back.

"Hi there," she said. "I'm Carolina, and I want to be your friend."

They breathed each other's air for a few seconds, and once she felt it was safe to touch her, Carolina stroked the mare's nose. She was soft beyond comparison. Carolina realized that behind the anxiousness and stress of the move, in her heart Velvet was just as soft as her nose and her name.

Carolina put her hand in her jacket pocket. Her fingers found the horse treat she'd grabbed before leaving the house. She looked around for a treat bucket.

She was rash, but not reckless. No matter how friendly or loving a horse was, it was never smart to feed them with bare hands. Their teeth are strong enough to tear out deep-rooted weeds. Velvet and Carolina were just starting to know each other. It was best to minimize risks.

Carolina couldn't see well in the semidarkness. Things were organized differently here. Finally, she found what she was looking for.

Velvet nickered again. This time it seemed she was asking where Carolina had gone.

"I'm here," she replied. "Coming."

The treat made a plinking sound when it fell in the shallow bucket.

"I know it's not the best, but it's all I have for now. But I promise you next time I'll bring you something yummier. Apples are in season, and Mom went to the market today. I think you'll like her. And the apples. This time of the year . . ."

She went on and on about apples and everything else that crossed her mind while Velvet chewed on her treat slowly. As if she sensed that once the last crumb was gone, Carolina would have to leave the barn.

Carolina watched her chew. She noticed Velvet's right hind leg was raised as if she were afraid to put any weight on it. But she also saw bandages expertly wrapped around it, which meant Dr. Rooney had been to see Velvet already. With his care and that of the rest of the staff, the horse's leg would heal. Carolina was certain. She'd do anything to help Velvet fit in at the ranch.

An owl hooted outside as if it had been a lookout for Carolina.

"I have to get going," she said, wishing she could stay with Velvet all night. "I'll come back tomorrow, my beauty."

She knew she had no right to call her *my beauty*. And she had no right to promise to be back in the morning. She had chores. Velvet belonged to Chelsie.

But the heart wants what it wants, and Carolina's was melting for Velvet.

She gave the mare a parting kiss on the nose.

"Bye, Velvet," she whispered.

Velvet nickered her goodbye.

Carolina walked back into the cold night. She made sure to latch the door and turned around to sprint back uphill, when a shadow streaked in front of her.

Carolina yelped, placing a hand on her drumming chest.

It was Luna, who stared at her unfazed.

There were no dogs at Paradise because dogs and horses don't always get along. But Luna had taken over the position of yard guardian. As if she had guessed Carolina's train of thought and wanted to prove her right, Luna tensed again and pounced on a moving shadow.

But shadows don't squeak, and this one was protesting loudly.

"Is that a mouse?" Carolina asked, trying not to gag. She felt bad for the poor mouse but also impressed with the cat's reflexes.

Lightning crisscrossed the sky.

With another storm approaching, the little creatures that roamed the night were frantically looking for a dry, warm spot to hunker down until the spring.

Carolina left Luna to feast on her morsel and ran to the cottage at the top of the hill.

Just in time too, because as soon as she closed the kitchen door behind her, thunder rumbled and made the windows rattle.

The pitter-patter of raindrops on the rooftop disguised the

sound of her tiptoeing upstairs. She stood by her window and took one last peek at the ranch. The lightning crisscrossing the dark sky reflected how conflicted she felt. She shouldn't have gone out without permission. Not in the middle of the night.

But then, no more scared neighing came from the big barn. She smiled. Some rules just had to be broken, if you had a good reason. Right?

7

Get Out of **My** Barn!

Saturday morning dawned cold and rainy. Carolina snuggled in the warmth of her bed. But images from her nighttime escapade rushed back to her. She'd promised her dad she would be obedient. She'd also promised Velvet she'd go back to visit her. How would she do both?

She'd have to figure it out after chores. Work and routine didn't change at the ranch, not even on holidays. No matter the day, the horses needed food and care. Maybe if she got done with chores early, then she could talk to Kimber about exchanging lessons for classes. She could even volunteer to help with Velvet.

The thought cheered her up and made her jump from bed to get ready.

She had a smile on when she went downstairs. The house was empty. Papi usually headed to the barn while it was still dark. Mom volunteered at the library on Saturdays. Carolina imagined that with the start of the new school year in less than two weeks, there would be a lot of excitement. The library could use all the help they could get.

Carolina rushed to do her house chores so she could finally get to the stable. On her way down the driveway, she saw Kimber riding a gray Arabian horse in the big outdoor arena even though the sky was overcast. The asphalt was speckled with sprinkling rain. The horse was spirited, but he obeyed her. Even from a distance she could tell that Kimber had complete control of the situation. Just like Tina Hodges in her videos. Except Kimber was here in front of her.

Carolina wanted to be just like her when she grew up.

She fantasized about all the things she still had to learn. When she arrived at the small barn, she stopped short at the entrance. She could feel a strange presence. Not ghostly or scary. Just the feeling that someone different had been here.

For one thing, the light was already on. She never left it on at night. It messed with the horses' sense of the seasons. She'd heard horror stories of winter coats not coming in on time for the cold weather because of bright lights in the stable.

When she looked around, her suspicions were confirmed. There was a clump of horsehair in the drain. Hay was scattered around the trash can, which was only for actual trash. Her cleaning supplies were all in the wrong place. And it looked like Twinkletoes was eating the wrong kind of feed! He was still on a special diet, Papi had said just the day before.

A different CD from the one she'd played the afternoon before was in the old boom box. She distinctly remembered choosing '90s classics instead of the early 2000s mix. The little hairs on the back of her neck prickled. Papi must have sent one of the new stable hands to do the morning chores today. But why? Did he think she couldn't do things on her own anymore? A feeling of defensiveness shivered through her. She'd done a great job the day before!

"Do you know who's been here, Luna?"

The barn cat blinked like a sphinx and swished her tail from side to side from her throne high in the rafters.

Carolina was going to find her dad in the big stable to ask about the mess in the little barn—but then she heard hushed voices coming from outside.

She tiptoed all the way to the back window, attempting not to make a sound. But the moment she tried to be as quiet as possible, her rubber boots squeaked.

She stood frozen for a second. The conversation outside continued.

No. Not a conversation. An argument—between Heather and Chelsie.

Carolina wondered if she should cough or play some music to alert them that they had an unexpected audience.

"It will be good for you," Heather said in a coaxing voice.

"How?" Chelsie's whining voice said. "With the storm, I didn't really sleep well last night. And I had to wake up extra early today! I still have jet lag from coming from California, Mom!"

"Farmwork requires early mornings. I warned you about it when I told you about my plans. You said yes to early mornings when we got Velvet."

"I didn't know how early horses wake up though," Chelsie said. "Besides, why am I here in this tiny barn with these little ponies and not there with her?"

Little ponies? Carolina scoffed. Leilani was a good-size horse, and Pepino was fourteen hands even, just a couple of inches short of the height that would designate him a horse instead of a pony.

But more to the point, was Chelsie talking about . . . the little barn? *She* had done the barn chores and left everything in the wrong place?

Carolina looked around and saw a yellow backpack hanging from one of the pegs at the entrance of the barn. Maybe Heather and Chelsie would come back in for it any second. Maybe Carolina shouldn't be here . . .

But it was *her* job to take care of the little barn. No one had told her otherwise.

First, she felt mad. Who was Chelsie to come in and do *her* work? And then a little voice of doubt chimed in. Who was Chelsie? The new owner—at least kind of. For the first time in her life, Carolina felt like maybe she didn't belong in Paradise.

She tried to keep her emotions at bay and reason the way Papi would.

True. Her family didn't own the ranch, but this was *her* home. Didn't that count for anything? Chelsie should've asked before she moved things around. But then, it sounded like maybe Heather had asked Chelsie to help, so she was probably doing what she was told.

And Chelsie did not sound happy about it.

Bella stared at Carolina, definitely judging her for eavesdropping.

Carolina narrowed her eyes and muttered, "Oh, shush, you!"

The mini horse whipped her mane to the side and turned to face the wall.

"This is how I learned a good work ethic, my love," Heather was saying. "At the barn with the horses."

Carolina knew she shouldn't eavesdrop, but what if Chelsie and her mom said something about Velvet? Or about the new lesson clinic Heather was supposedly planning? Or about Chelsie taking over the little barn?

No. She had to listen. This was her home, and she had the right to know what she was up against. She belonged here. Right?

"But I want to be riding," Chelsie replied to her mom. "Not cleaning. Isn't that why we have staff? What's the point of paying all these people? I don't want to pick up horse poop. I didn't come here to be a pooper scooper."

Pooper scooper.

A rush of heat went all the way from Carolina's tiptoes to the crown of her head. Her attempts to reason galloped out the window as the words brought her back to a day early in the summer.

Loretta and Tessa had been ready to leave the big barn after their lesson when Carolina reminded them to clean up after their horses. She wasn't being bossy. It was common sense to pick up droppings, especially after she and her dad had just swept the whole barn.

The girls hadn't taken it well.

"Who does she think she is?" Tessa muttered as Carolina was walking away.

"Well, what do you expect from the *official* pooper scooper?" Loretta said, not even trying to lower her voice.

They had laughed so hard, they startled Loretta's horse. Carolina had whipped around, a fire sparking in her chest. They thought they could call her names and then leave Loretta's poor horse in a dirty stall? She tried to channel her mom's teacher voice. "Excuse you? What did you just say?"

Her sharp tone worked. Loretta and Tessa stopped laughing. Tessa scrambled to get the rake hanging from a hook on the wall. But Loretta, flush faced, smirked at Carolina.

She planted a hand on her hip. "Thanks, Tessa. You're a real friend," she said, her expression clearly implying that Carolina wasn't.

"No problem, Lori," Tessa said, hurling the droppings to the manure container and leaving the rake leaning against the stall door.

They left through the other exit, yelling "pooper scooper" once they were out of sight.

Still fuming, Carolina placed the rake carefully where it belonged and gave poor Poseidon a treat and a pat on his nose.

Ever since, Carolina hadn't spoken to Loretta and Tessa.

She didn't mind her job. She loved it. She took to heart everything Papi said about true horsemanship and caring for the horses. But if she was being honest, she had to recognize that the mean words hurt. To hear them now from Chelsie's lips meant she was one of *those* girls. Carolina was crushed. But at least she knew. And see? Her hunch had been right. It was better to know now before she made a fool of herself trying to become friends. Chelsie didn't deserve that second chance after all.

Heather surprised her when she sighed and said, "Chels . . . I wish you wouldn't say those things. I regret that you spent so much time with Aunt Bernice last year. I hoped you wouldn't fall for her ideas of who belongs where depending on what they own."

"I thought you loved her." Chelsie's voice had a hint of surprise and accusation.

"I do. I love her with all my heart and I'll be forever grateful for all she did for us. I miss her every day. She made it possible for us to have this beautiful land and the horses. It's been my dream all my life to own a ranch like this. But she had very wrong ideas about race and class that I hope she didn't pass on to you."

Carolina's mind whirled with questions.

Who was this Aunt Bernice? And how had she helped Ms. Whitby have the money to buy this property?

"I'm sorry, Mom," Chelsie mumbled. Carolina wished she could see her face to tell if she was sincere.

"I want you to learn that the value of a person doesn't depend on outward appearances or possessions. Or social positions. Those labels don't mean anything! That little girl, Jen and Amado Aguasvivas's daughter, has more work ethic than any other person Great-Aunt Bernice might have been friends with. Or some of the horses' owners who treat their animals like little toys instead of creatures with their own feelings and thoughts."

"Daddy said that too once," Chelsie said. "I miss him. I wish . . ."

Carolina held her breath to hear what Chelsie was about to say.

"I wish I were with him."

The silence that followed was painful. Carolina didn't even like Chelsie, but she felt a twinge of pity for her.

Then Heather said, "I'm sorry you feel that way. Hopefully our grand experiment will work. You seemed happy with Velvet. Have you changed your mind?"

"No!" Chelsie said, her response like a whip.

"In that case, you have to put in your fair share of work. Or as much as you can do. I want the new riding clinic to start as soon as possible, and I want things to start on the right note. The first rule is that if you're going to ride, you need to muck the stalls. That's final."

There was an uncomfortable silence.

Carolina couldn't help it: She felt some satisfaction in hearing Chelsie being told off.

Heather continued, "I already talked to Mr. Aguasvivas. He said that you and Carolina can help each other at the little barn."

Not the little barn! She didn't want Chelsie taking over her space.

"What about school?" Chelsie asked.

School, schmool, Carolina thought. Chelsie was in for a rude awakening to what life on a ranch entailed. There was no recess. No summer or winter breaks. No rest.

"What about it?" Heather asked.

"School starts in nine days, Mom."

"The answer is the same. If you want to ride Velvet or any other horse, then you will report to the barn every morning before school."

"But—"

"Chels, once you prove you're dependable at the barn, you will be able to start riding Velvet."

"That's not fair!" Chelsie exclaimed, and Carolina heard

the stomping of a foot. It didn't sound any less obnoxious in expensive boots.

"You need to connect with Velvet if you want to go to competitions and shows next year. The sign-ups close on September seventh. That's less than three weeks. Velvet's very talented and has a lot of potential, but I won't take any risks if she's not ready."

"I want to compete," Chelsie said.

"Maybe on another horse," Heather replied. "Maybe with the other horse Kimber has been training, Shadow."

"I don't want another horse, Mom. And how will I connect with Velvet if I'm at this barn and she's over there all alone? She hardly knows me!"

"All the work you do here will show out there in the arena and the other barn. I promise. You'll see."

Chelsie didn't say anything, but Carolina felt the tension in the air. So did the horses, judging by their jitters.

Heather broke the silence. "Carolina must be arriving any time. Go in and see what she needs you to do."

Carolina was confused. Heather wanted Carolina to tell Chelsie what to do?

"According to every other person at the ranch, she's always on time and incredibly competent for her age," Heather continued. "It'll do you well to follow her example."

Carolina hated comparisons. She felt proud Heather had such a high opinion of her, but at the same time, she was sure getting compared to her would not make Chelsie like her more.

"Okay," Chelsie said at last.

"See you later, honey."

"Bye," Chelsie replied.

Carolina felt guilty for eavesdropping. But she had good reason to. Now she knew what kind of person Chelsie was.

She was indignant that Chelsie thought she was too good for mucking stalls. She grabbed the broom and started sweeping the stall around Bella. New owner or not, she'd show this girl what true horsemanship was all about.

8

Let's Get to Work

Carolina came face-to-face with Chelsie in the entrance to the small barn.

"Hey," she said. Her voice sounded stiff and cold. She wasn't a pretender and the pooper scooper comment still stung.

Chelsie didn't smile either. "Hey." She crossed her arms and looked around the barn with that infuriating upturned nose, but her cheeks were a bright red.

Could she tell that Carolina had overheard the argument with her mom?

"My mom says I'll start doing the morning chores from now on."

"*I* can do them," Carolina snapped. She would actually be

doing Chelsie a favor. She didn't want to be a *pooper scooper* after all.

Chelsie's jaw hardened. "Your dad said it's a lot of work for one girl. Every day, twice a day. It becomes a lot. Especially with school starting soon."

"I know what I can handle." Carolina rolled her eyes. "I've been helping with the little barn chores for two years. I like it."

"I . . ." Chelsie said, and for a second Carolina thought the girl would lie and say she liked it too. But instead, Chelsie added, "I can learn." She squared her shoulders. "My mom says I have to, so you *have* to teach me."

Carolina didn't want to be like Chelsie, all *my mom this, your dad that.* But even though she couldn't stand to think it, Carolina knew her dad was right. She hadn't ever had to do all the work on her own. And though Chelsie didn't know it, Carolina had heard Heather herself. It didn't sound like either of them was getting out of this arrangement. But maybe . . . maybe she could stay in charge.

"I have a system all set up. It took me a while to learn how to do all the tasks. You'll have to pay attention," she finally said.

Chelsie sighed but she nodded.

It was obvious they'd both rather be doing anything other than working together.

But at least Carolina was the one bossing Chelsie around instead of the other way.

"You can shadow me today so tomorrow morning you'll have a better idea of what to do. I guess you *tried* to muck the stalls," Carolina said, noticing how cutting her words sounded but unable to stop them. "You need to move the horses out first though."

"My mom tried to help me out, but she had to run back to the office. Lots of things to do," Chelsie said. "Andrew and JC are showing her the ropes around the big barn."

"I thought she wanted to do everything in a new way," Carolina said.

Chelsie shrugged. "There's no need to reinvent the wheel," she said with a voice that sounded just like her mom's.

Maybe not everything at the ranch would change dramatically. Carolina's shoulders relaxed just a smidge.

"Good. When my dad said something about winds of

change, I wasn't expecting a hurricane to go through the little barn."

Chelsie didn't laugh at the joke.

"It's a lot of work, Chelsie," Carolina said, trying to make her voice sound kind and pleasant, and yet direct. She knew she shouldn't hurt Chelsie's feelings on purpose. Plus, she didn't want to offend Heather . . . or put Papi's job in jeopardy.

But the truth was if Chelsie couldn't keep up with her chores, then someone else would have to pick up the slack. And that someone would either be Papi or Carolina.

Chelsie puffed up her chest and said, "I can learn."

There was no other choice but to teach Chelsie what she knew. "Okay, then. Let's get started," Carolina said. "Do you want to grab the other broom?"

Chelsie grabbed the broom, but it looked like she didn't even know how to hold it. She started to *brush* it lightly over the concrete floor. After watching her in horror for a couple of moments, Carolina suggested, "Actually, why don't you take Bella back to the pasture for now, and then come back for Pepino and the rest. Then we can clean out the stalls."

"But it's raining," Chelsie said. "Horses don't like the rain."

"It's sprinkling," Carolina countered. "And some of them do. At least, when it's just misting. There's a small shelter in the pasture. They know what to do."

"And what are *you* going to do?" asked Chelsie.

So much for teamwork. Carolina already felt ruffled. "I'll be sweeping and hosing the stalls. Is that okay with you?" She almost added *Your Majesty* and a curtsy, but she thought better of it.

Still, her intentions must have been plain on her face.

Chelsie muttered something to Bella and led her back to the pasture. The traitor mini horse swished her tail from side to side and gave Carolina a sideways glance that made her shake her head. The little stinker! Was she trying to make Carolina jealous?

Carolina was determined to leave the stall sparkling, setting the bar so high Chelsie would have a hard time keeping up the next morning.

But Chelsie surprised her.

She was back in no time for the rest of the horses. Then she grabbed a broom and imitated Carolina. She must have gotten warm because she took off her fancy fringed jacket and tried to hook it next to the saddles.

"It's going to fall right into that puddle. Why don't you try those coat hangers where you left your backpack?" Carolina said, pointing at the row of pegs next to the door. "The first one's mine though," she added.

Chelsie didn't protest as she moved the backpack and placed her jacket on the last peg, as far from Carolina's as she could.

She grabbed the broom once again, and slowly but surely, she finally got the hang of sweeping.

The two girls scrubbed and mopped in silence. Chelsie went slowly but steadily, Carolina fast and efficiently. In other circumstances, she would've been singing to her heart's content, but she didn't feel comfortable doing it with Chelsie right there.

It wasn't the same with a stranger in the barn. Especially a stranger who'd never swept a floor, by the looks of it.

Soon, the space smelled of eucalyptus and lemon instead of manure.

As they stashed their brooms, Chelsie looked around with a satisfied expression on her face, but then she frowned. "Oh, you left some hay behind."

"No, I didn't—" Carolina said, but she stopped when she saw that it was true. She'd left a trail of hay from one corner of the barn to Leilani's stall. Chelsie swept it into the stall and shut the door.

Carolina shrugged. "Thanks." The word was hard to say, but she would try her hardest not to be rude. No matter how she felt about Chelsie.

But Chelsie didn't cooperate. She didn't even say a simple "you're welcome." Instead, the scowl was back on her face. As if she were doing Carolina a favor and not the other way around!

"Okay, then. If that's all, I'm out of here," Chelsie said, grabbing her things. "Bye."

"Whatever," Carolina said, shrugging. She made a point of straightening up the broom that Chelsie had put back in the holder.

They each went their separate ways. Although Carolina had

said *thank you* politely and tried to be nice, Chelsie's cold attitude made her feel like she'd done something wrong.

Hoping to catch a glimpse of Velvet, Carolina went the long way back to the cottage, the one that took her past the fancy barn and the big outdoor ring.

The rain had stopped, but there were a few puddles in the arena. To her delight, Carolina spotted Velvet's sleek coat, darkened by the light rain.

Kimber was doing groundwork with her, a resolute expression on her face as Velvet circled her. The mare galloped at a chaotic rhythm, and her circle around the trainer was wobbly and uneven. Kimber kept trying to push her farther out.

Velvet tossed her mane, unwilling to comply judging by the glint of rebellion in her eyes.

She was so beautiful, Carolina's breath caught.

A leaf blower thundered from around the corner, and Velvet spooked at the sound, twisting this way and that. Kimber tried to get her attention, but the mare was too distracted. Her ears swiveled nervously. At least her leg seemed okay.

What else was bothering Velvet? Why did she look so unhappy?

Before Carolina headed back to the cottage, she realized that on the exact opposite side of the arena, Chelsie was watching Velvet too.

Her face reflected the longing to solve the mystery of Velvet that throbbed in Carolina's heart. But unlike Carolina, who had no right to spend time with the mare, Chelsie walked into the arena and helped Kimber lead Velvet back to the big barn.

That night, when they met for nighttime chores, they didn't exchange a word. This time, Chelsie hung up her jacket on her designated hook without being told.

The unease settled into Carolina's stomach and didn't even let up when she repeated her midnight visit to the big barn. Velvet ate the apple she brought in two sharp bites.

9

Oops!

For the next several days, Carolina showed up at the little barn a bit earlier than usual to beat Chelsie to it. She also snuck out late every night to bring apples for Velvet. Soon, the late nights and early mornings caught up with her. But she couldn't stop.

She didn't want Chelsie to take over her chores, and the mare was still not making a lot of progress. Or at least not in her behavior. Her leg seemed a lot better, but she was still skittish when she worked with Kimber. The trainer insisted no one would ride her yet.

Usually after her evening chores, Carolina watched some of the training sessions, but she couldn't see what Kimber was trying to accomplish. Apparently, neither could Velvet. Carolina was convinced that if *she* had the chance to work with her, Velvet would improve.

She had a magical touch with horses after all, didn't she?

If only that magical ability to make friends with horses transferred to making friends with people.

One day, Chelsie had left the ranch with Loretta and Tessa after their lesson. Carolina hadn't even seen them leave. She'd heard about it later when Chelsie told Kimber that they wanted to switch and take lessons with her instead of the trainer from Boise. She just said "we," and it meant her, Loretta, and Tessa.

Ever since, the tension between Chelsie and Carolina had increased. Every time Carolina tried to talk to her, she remembered how Chelsie had scoffed at working in the little barn, and the desire to reach out left her. Chelsie didn't do anything to try to change Carolina's mind.

Carolina could imagine Loretta, Tessa, and Chelsie talking about her. She had seen the three of them laughing. Were they laughing at her? Chelsie didn't seem shy with them.

Carolina couldn't stand the thought that while Chelsie

wasted time with those girls, Velvet was in her stall all alone. How was the mare supposed to get better?

Time was running out. The first day of school was the next day. September seventh and the sign-up deadline for the competition was less than two weeks away. Carolina could hear a ticking clock thundering in her mind, but it seemed she was the only one who cared about Velvet's future.

Carolina arrived at the barn a whole hour earlier than usual, bundled up against the chilly air. Chelsie had never really noticed that Carolina was trying to beat her to chores every morning. But this time when she arrived, there wasn't much left to do.

"I guess you can brush Bella," Carolina said with a dismissive shoulder shrug when Chelsie asked what her chores were. "You know how to do that, don't you?"

Chelsie lifted her chin defiantly. "Of course I do."

"Sweet," Carolina said, and headed out.

As she was heading back to the cottage, she saw Kimber heading out to the back trail with her own horse, Sadie. The two looked like one creature, a centaur, two halves of the same heart. It was a beautiful thing to see.

Carolina sighed. She hoped that one day, she and her soul mate horse would go on rides like that. But for now, any other horse would do. Not on the trail, or at least not those where her dad sometimes took tourists. Just the little deer paths around the property. Her dad usually let her ride there on her own. Maybe she could meet Kimber when the instructor came back.

With this thought in mind, she ran home to change from her chores outfit into riding clothes. She didn't own special breeches or fancy gloves, but her well-worn jeans and boots would do.

She headed out to the pasture to fetch Leilani. Pepino wasn't happy that his friend was leaving without him, and he threw a fit of Pepino proportions, tossing his mane and stomping his hoof once.

"Oh, for goodness' sakes, Pep!" Carolina said. "You'll be able to still see us from where you stand."

Pepino didn't seem convinced, but when Twinkletoes came up to him, he calmed down a little. Together, they headed to lick their salt block in the middle of the dried-up clover field.

"You're such a good friend, Twinkles," Carolina said, making a mental note to bring him a treat of some kind later.

She had hoped that Chelsie would be done grooming Bella when she came back, but to her surprise, when she went inside the little barn to tack up Leilani, she found that there was music playing, something funny and energetic in a language she didn't recognize. In the big double stall, Chelsie sat on a stool braiding Bella's tail.

The two girls pretended not to see each other, but there was so much tension in the barn that Leilani got nervous.

"Easy," Carolina said as she placed the heavy saddle on the horse. Horses can't hold their breath, but Leilani kept tightening her abdomen, making it impossible for Carolina to pull the cinch tight enough. She tried a couple of times. The more she tried, the more aware she became of Chelsie's judgmental looks. Then the more nervous Leilani was, which led to her tightening her abdomen. It was a vicious cycle.

Carolina blew the strand of hair that kept falling across her face and ended up redoing her ponytail to put her helmet on. She had already worked up a sweat and she hadn't even sat on the saddle yet.

"Let's go," she said. "We'll fix it outside."

She led Leilani to the mounting block outside the barn, and in her eagerness to meet up with Kimber, she forgot to retighten the cinch, or at least check on it. From the corner of her eye, she saw Chelsie watching her while pretending not to notice anything, so she decided to pretend that everything was okay too.

She made a kissing sound and pressed her legs against Leilani's belly and the mare started walking toward the big arena.

"Not there today," Carolina said, and led her to the trail.

Leilani snorted.

Sweat prickled Carolina's armpits, scalp, and top lip. Everything felt wrong, even her own skin. She let out a big breath and tried to silence her doubts. Maybe it wasn't such a good idea to head to the trail on her own. Not when Leilani was so nervous for some reason.

But as she decided to head to the big arena instead, she saw Kimber and Sadie climbing down from the trail onto the gravel area behind the office building.

Kimber noticed her and waved. When Carolina lifted her hand to say hi, a squirrel ran across the path. Leilani may as well have seen a ghost. She didn't rear up, but she screamed and twisted to the right. Carolina's instincts kicked in, and she placed a calming hand on Leilani's neck as she whispered, "Shhh. It's just a squirrel, sweetheart."

Leilani continued backing up, and when she turned away from the sound of the squirrel scurrying through the leaves, the saddle began to tip out of place.

Carolina lost her balance and started to fall.

10

Unsaddled

Kimber and Sadie galloped to Carolina's side and reached her in seconds. Carolina had pitched herself hard away from her fall and clung on to Leilani's neck. The trainer took hold of the horse's reins. Kimber appeared calm, but there was a spark of alertness in her eyes.

"Are you okay?" she said.

Carolina was super embarrassed as she unsuccessfully tried to rebalance the saddle into place. "Yes, my cinch was loose, I guess."

As her heartbeat started to slow, she saw Chelsie standing by the little barn's entrance holding Bella by the lead rope. Bella's hair was intricately braided. She looked like a fairy pony. The miniature horse must have felt so loved and pretty that she even looked like she was smiling. But Chelsie's eyebrows rose as she looked at Carolina all lopsided on Leilani's back.

"Climb down. We're going to fix it," Kimber said, getting off her horse in an expert, swift move.

Carolina obeyed and got off the saddle knowing she didn't look nearly as graceful as the trainer.

"Here," Kimber said, handing her Sadie's reins.

The trainer got to work on straightening the saddle, whispering to Leilani that everything was okay.

The embarrassment over having to be rescued like this was so unbearable that Carolina had the urge to run away. For the first time in her life, she understood why horses run when they're spooked. She tended to confront things . . . like a donkey. Or a mule.

The whinny of a horse interrupted her thoughts. She turned around and saw Velvet in the big pasture backing away from two horses: the beautiful gray Arabian Kimber had been training for a new client and a sorrel quarter horse Carolina had never met before. JC and Papi stood by the fence watching the horses, but they didn't seem concerned.

But Carolina wasn't so sure that turning Velvet out with the rest of the pack had been a good idea. She needed less stress in her life, not more.

"Oh no," she said when she saw Velvet retreating farther into the pasture.

When Kimber lifted her gaze, she clicked her tongue. Sadie pawed at the ground, echoing Kimber's disappointment.

Velvet was standing as far away from the herd as possible, the picture of misery and loneliness.

"Should we go help her?" Carolina asked when Kimber went back to fixing the saddle on Leilani. She was ready to bolt and rescue Velvet from being bullied.

But Kimber was shaking her head. "They all need to sort out the pecking order of the herd."

"What if they hurt her?"

"Your dad and JC know what they're doing," she said. "You need to trust them."

She did trust them. But she didn't like to see Velvet struggling.

"Here," Kimber said, handing her Leilani's reins again. "She's set to go."

Carolina was trying to find the courage to ask if they could bring Velvet to the arena, when she saw Chelsie come out of the little barn with Pepino, all tacked up and ready to ride.

"Where are you going?" Carolina blurted out before she could stop herself.

At first she thought Chelsie hadn't heard her because the other girl didn't reply for a few long seconds. She just kept her gaze down as if studying the ground before she took each step. "What does it look like?" she finally said. "I'm taking Pepino to the arena for a ride."

"But I was going there with Leilani," Carolina protested.

"You can share the arena. It's a big space," Kimber said in a singsongy voice.

Carolina had never shared that ring with anyone else, but things had changed at the ranch. With so many new people around, everyone would have to share space. And she had no right to keep Chelsie away from any spot on the property anyway. Even the cottage at the top of the hill belonged to Chelsie and her mom. Even Pepino belonged to this new girl who'd swooped in and taken everything from Carolina, even her peaceful Sunday rides.

"Do you think Velvet would like to do some groundwork there with us?" Carolina said, her heart about to break through her chest.

"She's not ready yet," Chelsie replied, her scowl noticeable even though the helmet was too big for her and covered most of her face.

Kimber pressed her lips and nodded. "Exactly. Maybe one-on-one. But not with other horses around yet."

Carolina's galloping heart fell to her stomach.

Kimber seemed to notice her disappointment because she said, "Next time Chelsie and I work with her, we'll invite you. How about that?"

Carolina nodded. She wanted to be there, of course, but the fact that she had to be invited to be part of anything that was happening at the ranch left her with a sour taste in her mouth.

And judging by Chelsie's face, it was obvious the other girl wished the invite hadn't been extended at all.

Carolina did her best to smile and said, "Sure. Thanks for helping me with my saddle."

Kimber was already heading to the big barn. "Anytime!" she replied.

Carolina waited until Chelsie was already trotting laps around the arena with Pepino before she and Leilani joined them. Pepino and Leilani made eye contact each time they crossed, but the girls ignored each other.

Carolina noticed how careful and precise every one of Chelsie's moves was. She felt a rush of jealousy for her technique, but remembered that most likely, the other girl had hours and hours of more training than Carolina.

For the next while, they both pretended not to see each other—which took a lot more energy than Carolina ever imagined. Instead of feeling the usual exhilaration after a ride, she felt exhausted and . . . something else.

It was like the dread that had clawed at her stomach when she lost her balance on the saddle hadn't left.

Carolina felt *unsaddled*.

First she felt invaded in the little barn. Made fun of. And now? Now she was wasting energy ignoring Chelsie.

She hated the feeling.

"I'm sorry I wasn't a good sport tonight," she told Leilani after she put her back in the barn for the night. She'd waited until Chelsie had finished working with Pepino, who'd risked a jump, the little stinker. He'd never even tried with Carolina. Or maybe she hadn't known what he was capable of . . .

"I guess I have too many things on my mind."

Leilani just listened patiently. Carolina put extra care in brushing her and braided a tiny strand on the mare's mane. It wasn't as pretty as what Chelsie had done on Bella though, and again, her heart felt heavy.

Comparison is the thief of joy, her mom usually said, and today had been proof of that.

Chelsie's arrival had turned Carolina's world upside down. She didn't even want to imagine what things would be like when they started school the next day.

If only she could talk to Vida about everything that had

happened at the ranch since she'd left on her family vacation! With the fifteen-hour time difference to the Philippines, they could rarely video chat or message in real time. At first, they'd exchanged emails, but when the summer sun was bright and the prairie called her name, Carolina didn't have the patience to sit and write a long letter—or to wait for Vida's replies. It had been ages since they'd talked. When Vida had departed in July, they had both assumed Vida would be the one with the most things to share. Neither of them had imagined that Carolina's life would change so much with the arrival of the new owners.

For once, Carolina wished she could text her friend, even though she'd see her the very next day. Usually Carolina never felt the need to have a phone, and her parents refused to let her have one before she turned twelve—at least. And then she'd have to help pay for it when she'd rather spend every cent she earned or got for gifts on horse-riding lessons. The house phone depended on the internet connection, which usually was flickering and unstable.

Like her emotions and thoughts.

Carolina waited until the occupants of the cottage and the mansion house went to sleep. As was her habit now, she snuck into the big barn.

If only she could have the chance to connect with Velvet! But how was she going to if Kimber insisted on being the only one doing groundwork with her? It didn't make sense. To Carolina at least.

She wanted to try taking Velvet out of her stall, maybe for a short walk. She had a magic touch, everyone said that.

She's not ready yet. Chelsie's words rang in her ears.

When Velvet greeted her with an impatient toss of the head, the warnings grew louder.

Velvet seemed agitated. Maybe one of the other horses had hurt her after all.

Carolina wanted to comfort the poor animal, but the stall half door was too much of a barrier between them. Carefully, she opened it and stood inside the stall for a couple of seconds to gauge the mare's reaction.

Velvet sighed deeply, her nostrils flaring.

"I brought you some treats," Carolina said. "Leilani loved them, and she has the best taste. I hope you like them. I think you'd like Leilani and Pepino too. You saw them today. What did you think?"

She'd forgotten to grab a pail. Ignoring all her own training, she held her palm as flat as she could to offer Velvet her treat. Velvet's lips wuffled over her hand.

The rain pitter-pattered on the zinc roofs of the lean-to and the barn in a lullaby.

She was so eager to take Velvet out into the arena!

Maybe that's what Velvet needed? It was so peaceful at night. The sound of the rain would calm her. She pondered how and when she might be able to do it.

For about an hour, they sat in companionable silence, until Carolina couldn't keep her eyes open anymore.

"Maybe the other fancy horses will be nicer to you tomorrow, sweetheart," Carolina said softly, pressing her nose against Velvet's.

Velvet let out a resonant sigh, then Carolina left the barn, making sure she locked the door, and went back to her house.

She felt so clever that no one had discovered her yet. She couldn't wait to share her secret with Vida on the first day of school tomorrow.

11

Twisted Heart

When Carolina showed up for morning chores, she was shocked to see that everything had already been done. She inspected the stalls, but the horses' bedding had been replaced. The four of them looked happy and clean, other than the usual sprigs of hay on Twinkletoes's coat. Even worse, she was appalled to see that the little braid that she'd painstakingly weaved in Leilani's mane was undetectable in the myriad of others that had appeared since last night.

She couldn't help it: She felt resentful. And regretful. She recognized a little flash of pride that Chelsie had learned so much from her, sure. But now that the owner's daughter could take care of the barn by herself, there was no need for Carolina. How would she earn her lessons if she wasn't needed in the little barn?

Why had Chelsie taken this from her too?

She hugged Twinkletoes, who was the only one who didn't have any braids, but when she saw the little ribbon in his tail, like Eeyore's, she gasped, upset. "Not you too, Twinks!"

Her heart was twisted in a whole bunch of complicated feelings.

More than invaded, she felt kicked out of the little barn. Chelsie did everything better than she did.

The donkey just gave her an apologetic look and went back to his oats and apples. She quickly checked that the apple pieces weren't big enough to choke him, but she found nothing to object to.

"I don't want to lose you," she said, hanging on to the donkey's neck. She wasn't even embarrassed when a few tears escaped her eyes. The horses didn't judge her. They loved her even if the new girl was trying to make it look like Carolina was an extra, an unwelcome leftover from the life before when Paradise was just old Orchard. Paradise didn't seem to have space for her.

She couldn't indulge in feeling sorry for herself though. Time marched on, mercilessly. If she didn't hurry, she'd miss the bus. She really didn't want to start the year like this.

She ran up to the cottage and changed into her new school clothes: a different pair of jeans and a purple T-shirt that read *I prefer horses to people*. Excited, she ran back down the state road to the bus stop before her mom could ambush her for a first-day-of-school photo. Unlike her best friend, Mom would not approve of her T-shirt, but Carolina thought it was funny. And honestly true.

The morning had a touch of chill and she jumped in place to keep herself warm. She glanced around in case Chelsie joined her, but there was no sign of her rival. Which was probably for the best. Maybe the bus could be the one place she didn't have to worry about Chelsie messing things up for her.

First-day-of-school jitters jingled in Carolina's stomach. It felt worse than usual, being weighed down with the disappointment of feeling out of place in the barn. She tried to focus on the excitement of seeing her friends, especially Vida . . . but instead she found herself calculating how many days until the spring competition registration window closed. Less than two weeks to go before Velvet got shut out. And no progress with a rider.

Carolina skipped up the stairs of the bus alone when it rumbled up. Her favorite part of school was the ride there and back with her best friend. She was so ready to see Vida and update her about everything happening at Paradise.

Vida lived in town, and her grandpa was the elementary school principal. She refused to ride to school with him though, claiming that her relationship with the top authority wasn't a good look for her social life.

The truth was that Carolina and Vida had been waiting for sixth grade ever since kindergarten. Sixth graders were assigned to the last row of the bus, and this year, the two of them were the only sixth graders on this bus route. Caro slid onto the cold fake leather of the last row with a grin.

When the bus entered town, she jumped to her feet. There was Vida at the first stop with her cousin Cyrus.

"Hey, Caro," he called, joining his rambunctious fellow second graders in the first row.

"Hey, Cy," she said, beaming when she saw Vida with a new hairstyle—blue tips instead of pink—and dainty star earrings dangling from her ears. "You got your ears pierced!" she squealed as they hugged and jumped in place in the aisle.

"And you grew about five inches!" Vida said. "Oh my gosh, Caro! That shirt is so funny!"

Carolina beamed. Mission accomplished.

"Sit down, please," said the driver, Mr. Remington. But the second graders' excited chatter drowned out his voice.

Clutching Vida's hand, Carolina led her to the back row they'd been coveting for years. When she noticed the pretty blue polish contrasting against her own nails, short to the quick, Carolina pulled her hands back.

"Judging by your tan, you've been outdoors a lot." Vida smiled. "You look radiant."

Carolina felt a rush of relief. With other people, there was no knowing how they'd changed over the summer. But Vida was as kind and bright as ever.

When Carolina was little, Loretta had been her best friend.

Things between them started changing before fifth grade when Loretta came back from summer camp in Idaho Falls. Suddenly, she and Tessa became inseparable. The "pooper scooper" comment this summer had put a permanent end to any hopes Carolina might have had of making up.

But Vida wasn't like that. She didn't care that she and Carolina had opposite interests. Their friendship transcended differences.

Why had it been so hard for Carolina to click with Chelsie when they even lived at the same place and had one objective in mind—to help Velvet? She didn't get it.

Vida must have felt there was something wrong because she said, "So, I hear there's been an avalanche of changes up at the ranch. Spill." She took out a knitting project from her pink backpack.

"Since when do you knit?" Carolina asked in awe, staring at the rainbow string that weaved into a swath of material.

"My cousin Francine taught me as soon as I arrived in Manila. It's very relaxing."

Carolina shrugged. She didn't understand how her friend could be so talented. Or how Vida could even think knitting was relaxing. It looked complicated and time-consuming. "What are you making?"

"Not sure yet," Vida said. "Now, tell me. We don't have a lot of time."

"I couldn't bear to sit down and write everything to you—but so much has happened!" Carolina gushed. Vida's needles flashed and clinked as Carolina told her the events of the last couple of weeks. With every word that came to the tip of her tongue, she had to fight the urge not to say anything unfair about Chelsie. Carolina's parents didn't like gossip.

Vida had the perfect reaction to every bit of news Carolina added.

"Oooh," she said, her eyes lighting up. "I love the name Paradise." And then when Carolina told her about Chelsie and how she was taking over all the chores, she said, "I wondered if she would be on the bus too?"

"Me too," Carolina said. "There was no sign of her this morning though."

"Well, it's her first day at a new school," Vida said. "Her mom must have wanted to drive her." She glanced up and checked out the window, and quickly put her knitting back in her bright pink backpack. "It must be hard to be starting the last year of elementary and not really know anyone. We need to find her and show her around. Okay, Caro?"

"Sure," she said with a shrug. "I warn you though, she already met Loretta and Tessa. Apparently, they're friends."

Vida sighed. "Maybe they clicked because they all compete in shows?" Like always, she tried to see the bright side to every situation.

"Maybe." Carolina shrugged, hugging her utilitarian messenger bag, which was covered in patches in the shapes of horses. Her favorite one was a bright rainbow unicorn Vida had brought her from the Philippines last year. Carolina wished it were a real horse comforting her.

The bus slowed to a stop and the little kids jumped to their feet, ready to be the first ones to storm through the school doors.

There were so many more things Carolina had wanted to

tell her friend before she met Chelsie, but they had run out of time.

The bus lined up by the curb and Cyrus ran to join his friends. The second graders were chasing each other, strings of red and blue paper hanging from their waistlines. One boy had a bottle of water in the crook of his elbow, and he handed Cyrus a ribbon. Flag football, Carolina guessed. She smiled at how inventive and resourceful the little kids were.

She and Vida watched them, amused, until a black SUV pulled up to the curb.

"Is that . . . ?" Vida asked.

It was Chelsie! Even from the sidewalk, Carolina could see Chelsie's jaw was clenched as she looked at the world through her dark sunglasses. The frames were bright pink and covered with crystals that threw sparkles when Chelsie moved her head. She was so pretentious!

Kimber sat at the wheel, and Carolina wondered why Ms. Whitby hadn't driven her daughter to school.

Loretta and Tessa ran to meet Chelsie just as the bell rang. Loretta grabbed the sunglasses from Chelsie and tried them on.

"My turn now!" Tessa said, trying to snatch the glasses from Loretta, who held them up, out of Tessa's reach. Chelsie smiled tightly but didn't say anything. Carolina suppressed an eye roll.

"I have to stop by the office first," Vida said. "See you inside!"

Carolina gave her a thumbs-up and turned her back toward Chelsie and the growing group of girls surrounding the new girl on the sidewalk. She was patiently waiting to go inside the building when something hard hit her in the head. A feeling of cold wetness trickling down her back spread all the way to the top of her pants.

Some of the kids around her gasped.

A little in shock, Carolina tentatively touched the back of her head. Her hair was kind of matted. She'd washed it the night before, but she could have done a better job with the conditioner so this morning it would be easier to brush. Her head seemed okay, but wet.

"Are you okay?" asked a girl she didn't know.

Carolina didn't know what had just happened. Until she

saw the boy run toward her and grab the water bottle from her feet where it had landed. The wet sensation trickling down her back was water. He must have thrown the bottle he'd been carrying around like a football and hit her. But what if he'd hit a smaller kid?

Cyrus stood next to the boy, looking appalled. "Sorry, Caro."

The back of her head now throbbed with the impact as she tried to figure out what to say. She was embarrassed, but it had been an accident.

"It's okay," she finally said. "You all need to be careful with throwing bottles though."

The boy nodded, his eyes downcast. "Sorry," he said in a raspy voice. When he looked up at Carolina, his blue eyes were filled with tears.

Carolina smiled and was about to say something when someone tapped her on the shoulder. She turned around to see Loretta standing in front of her.

"Hey," Carolina said, surprised to see her standing so close to her. Maybe she was going to help her? Try to make peace with her?

But all her wishful thinking evaporated when Loretta spoke.

"Hey, that's my little brother. Be careful how you talk to him, pooper scooper," Loretta said with a sneer on her face and her hands on her hips.

A clamor of laughter erupted from most of the kids on the sidewalk. Chelsie didn't laugh. But she just stood behind Loretta, shoulders hunched all the way up to her ears.

"He hit me with a bottle," Carolina said, her temper rising.

Loretta snickered. "It was about time you got a bath," her voice boomed. No doubt everyone else heard her words, but no one said anything. "No wonder Ms. Whitby's new ranch manager didn't want to drive you in her car. You always stink of horses."

Carolina's cheeks started burning.

"My dad's still the ranch manager."

Loretta pursed her lips and shrugged. "Not for long," she said in a singsongy voice.

Carolina searched for Chelsie to tell the truth. There was a struggle reflected on Chelsie's face. It looked like she wanted to correct Loretta, but . . .

Why didn't she? Was she scared of Loretta? What kind of friendship was that?

Carolina wasn't afraid of anyone. The words tumbled out of her. "If you have something to say about my dad, say it to my face, Loretta." Her chin jutted out in a challenge as she turned toward Chelsie. "Well? What would your mom say about—"

Before Carolina could say *Chelsie's mom* wouldn't let her ride unless she too cleaned the stalls, Vida's grandfather, Principal Jones, came out. "The bell rang a long time ago, sixth graders!" he called. "Don't pretend you're all too grown-up to be at your desks on time!"

The students, led by Loretta and Tessa, rushed around the principal to head to the classroom. No one told Mr. Jones what had just happened.

"Let's go, Aguasvivas. And please hang your jacket on a hook to dry, child. Your mom won't be happy to know you got all wet playing before school. Should we call her to bring a dry outfit?"

Carolina bit her lip. There was no way she'd call her mom

and add school problems to her list of troublemaking. "No, thanks, Mr. Jones," she said, hating how her lip was quivering. "Sorry. I'll be more careful next time."

Mr. Jones nodded and, without another word, headed in.

Carolina followed him, but before she walked through the school doors, she sniffed under her armpits. Knowing she didn't smell bad at all was only a small consolation. But it was something.

· U ·

Carolina didn't tell Vida about the incident outside the school. When she walked into homeroom, she was relieved to see that Chelsie wasn't in her class. Maybe she and Loretta and Tessa had clicked so well that they'd requested to be placed together. Which was for the best. Having to see her at the ranch constantly was already too hard.

They finally crossed paths at lunch.

At their usual table with a bunch of girls from their class, Vida was gushing about the best halo-halo she'd ever had. "No shaved ice in America can compare to—" She stopped midsentence.

Carolina followed her gaze and saw Chelsie making her way through the cafeteria looking like a cowgirl lost in a blizzard. Her eyes found Carolina, who looked away. She didn't want to sit with her at lunch. Chelsie had taken over the ranch. She wouldn't let her take over her friend group.

But she shouldn't have worried.

"There you are!" Tessa called out to Chelsie from the table next to them. "Sorry we left you behind! We wanted to make sure no one else took our table."

Chelsie didn't say a word. She just sat between Loretta and Tessa, who exchanged a look like they'd won a blue ribbon.

"Remember, you don't want to sit with the pooper scooper anyway," Tessa pretended to whisper, but her voice was loud enough for the whole cafeteria to hear.

Carolina's ears rang. Anger like lava threatened to come out of her mouth in the form of mean words. She took a deep breath and counted to three. She didn't want to let those girls see that they'd hurt her.

But her intentions weren't enough to hold her own temper in check. "You haven't told them where you spend your mornings and evenings, have you, *Chels?* Maybe it's time your friends knew I'm not the only pooper scooper in Paradise. Don't you think?"

Carolina saw hurt cross her eyes for just a second. But Chelsie didn't reply. Loretta and Tessa exchanged a charged look. When they seemed to realize Chelsie wasn't going to explain, they changed the subject back to Chelsie's sunglasses.

"Do you think the pink matches my beanie?" Tessa asked, trying the sunglasses on top of her hat.

Carolina turned her back to them, still fuming.

"Yikes. Where did that come from?" Vida said, raising her eyebrows.

"I couldn't help it," she replied, crossing her arms, flustered. "She had it coming."

"Maybe you shouldn't have called her a pooper scooper," Vida said in a soft voice. "I mean, don't get me wrong. I'm one hundred percent on your side. But you hate it when Loretta and Tessa call you that. Besides, you and Chelsie live on the same property. I thought you'd be friends."

Carolina shrugged. Maybe Vida was right. Maybe she

should've been more gracious. But she was hurting, and she couldn't pretend. Not like other people.

That's why she preferred horses. They didn't lie or pretend. They always showed their true feelings. What they wanted. What they feared. And they only offered love.

If only people were as easy to deal with as horses!

12

Electric Charge

After school, Carolina and Chelsie arrived at the little barn at the same time. Neither one mentioned how Chelsie had beaten her to the barn that morning, or the confrontation outside the school or in the cafeteria. In fact, they didn't exchange a single word. They both pretended the other one wasn't there.

How long could the tension between them last before something snapped?

Somehow it held through the next few days. Even though they saw each other in the barn and at school, the silence between Carolina and Chelsie continued. Carolina began to feel the clock ticking. Did no one else feel the urgency to help Velvet so she could be ready for the sign-up date?

But on Thursday, her mood changed when Kimber popped inside the little barn and said, "I've been waiting for you to arrive. Do you want to come help me with Velvet?"

Both Carolina and Chelsie exclaimed, "Yes!"

Chelsie's eyes flew to Carolina, her face stony and cold. It was clear Chelsie didn't think Carolina should be included.

Carolina felt a knot grow in her throat. She'd thought Kimber was inviting both of them. Now she felt silly for having assumed . . .

"Sorry," she said in a small voice, looking at Kimber.

Kimber smiled. "No need to be sorry at all! I meant for both of you to come along. I told you I'd invite you next time, remember?"

Carolina's spirits soared like an eagle, while Chelsie looked like she'd rather keep doing chores than share Velvet with Carolina. But she didn't say anything as the three of them headed to the arena.

Carolina was so giddy with enthusiasm that she was practically skipping. At least something good was happening this week. She tried to listen attentively as Kimber explained the techniques she was using with Velvet. But Carolina was also distracted by Chelsie, who hung on behind them. She was quiet, but her body language spoke volumes.

She didn't want Carolina there.

Kimber seemed to notice because she looked over her shoulder and said, "Everything okay, Chels?"

Chelsie faked a smile. "Yep."

Carolina chose to ignore her bad attitude. And when she saw Velvet, she broke into a grin. "Hi, Velvet!"

Velvet was hitched to the patience pole. She tried to shake her head, but the rein was too short, poor thing. She couldn't really move her head more than a few inches, which was the whole point of the exercise.

"Aw!" Carolina said, and hurried toward the mare.

"Why is she tied up there?" Chelsie asked.

Kimber laughed. "Don't feel bad for her, Chels! The patience pole is a good way for her to absorb new exercises, to ground herself. We even had a short ride around the arena today, so she needed the alone time."

"You took her on a ride!" Carolina exclaimed loudly. She

tried to pat Velvet's nose, but the mare tried to move her face away.

"Careful, Caro," Kimber said softly.

"She was all calm before you got here," Chelsie said, standing between Carolina and Velvet. "You're ruining all of Kimber's work. Can't you see?"

"You're the one ruining *everything*." Carolina's enthusiasm fizzled like a popped balloon. "I just was excited that she went on a ride. That's all."

Kimber unclipped Velvet from the post and, holding her reins, took her in a wide circle to stretch her legs.

"Let me try!" said Chelsie, and grabbed the reins.

"Careful," said Carolina, her arms crossed, standing several feet away.

She was itching to take a turn, but Chelsie was right there standing in the way.

Velvet wasn't having any of it though. It was true she'd been behaving at the patience pole, but perhaps the animosity between the girls had affected her too much. Even when

Kimber took the reins out of Chelsie's hand, Velvet was jittery and distracted.

"Let's head to the arena," Carolina suggested, but when she reached the doorway, she saw JC was working with the Arabian horse. It looked like they'd be there a while.

Besides, Velvet looked like she'd had enough for the day.

"Sorry, girls. I didn't realize the arena was occupied," Kimber said. "We'll try again tomorrow."

"*I'll* come in the morning right after chores," Chelsie said, making sure Carolina understood there was no room for her.

"We just need to be patient with her," Kimber said. "Time will tell." She sounded so concerned for Velvet that she didn't seem to notice the wordless battle raging between the two girls.

Time was exactly what they didn't have. September seventh was just around the corner, and Velvet couldn't even go on a simple walk without becoming agitated.

Kimber took Velvet back to her stall, and Chelsie followed them. But this time, they didn't invite Carolina to come along.

She watched them go, trying to swallow her disappointment, but it sat in her chest like a rock.

· ∪ ·

That night, Carolina couldn't sleep.

She tried to distract herself by watching YouTube videos with the volume way down so she wouldn't wake her parents. Tina Hodges, the famous horse trainer from Wyoming, had posted a new video today.

She was training a mare that looked just like Velvet. They even both had the same defiant attitude. Carolina was in awe of Tina's calm manners and movements. She studied the trainer's every gesture, even how she stepped as she approached the skittish horse. Tina used a training whip, but not to hit the horse, just to use it as an extension of her arms. With her dark hair and the whip, the trainer reminded Carolina of a superheroine. Soon, the horse and the woman fell into a sequence that looked like they were dancing. At the end, the horse lowered its head and walked up to Tina, ready to ride.

Carolina imagined herself and Velvet going through the

groundwork sequences, connecting, bonding . . . just the two of them.

When the video was over, she clicked on repeat one, two, three times until she felt she had memorized the whole thing. It didn't look that hard. Maybe . . . maybe it wasn't hard at all. Carolina did have a magic touch after all, and she and Velvet had a special connection.

The temptation to go down to the big barn was too strong to resist. Velvet would be waiting for her. Nothing bad had happened on any of the nights she'd snuck into the barn in the last couple of weeks. The mare trusted her. She needed someone to help her feel at home here at Paradise. Carolina couldn't fail her. She would only visit her . . .

Unable to ignore the tug of her heart, she got up from her bed. The hardwood floor was cold on her feet although the heater was on, and she shivered. Carolina got dressed, ignoring the warnings in her mind, and headed out of the house as quietly as possible.

The gravel crunched under Carolina's boots. An owl hooted

from a nearby tree, and the bushy tail of a fox flashed through scraggly bushes. The owl and the fox wouldn't tell her off for sneaking out of her house. But in case there were other creatures or people out watching her progress down the lane, she tried to stick to the shadows.

She opened the gate. The scent of horses was like a warm hug, and she tiptoed all the way to Velvet's stall.

The mare seemed to have been waiting for Carolina. All the other horses were quiet and dozing, but Velvet was wide-awake and alert, her nostrils flaring. A plume of steam swirled in the air of the cold night. She pawed on the hay. The scent of urine tickled Carolina's nose.

"Hi, Velvet," Carolina whispered. Her voice echoed against the walls of the barn.

Velvet nickered softly, and Carolina put the treat she'd brought into Velvet's feed bucket.

She hadn't been planning to do anything other than visit. But how could she help Velvet without working with her? She knew that if she could help Velvet trust people again, she'd make a great horse for competitions and shows. Then Chelsie would feel so bad that she hadn't stood up for Carolina!

"Do you want to come out and play a little?" Her heart drummed in her ears. The annoying voice screamed that this was a big rule she was about to break. She could still turn back and go to bed.

Carolina looked at the animal's big brown eyes. For a second, she wondered if the hurt and fear she saw in them were a reflection of what was going on in Velvet's heart or her own.

There had been too many changes in the poor mare's life: new stable, new time zone, new food. There had been a lot of changes in Carolina's too: Her home didn't feel like home anymore. She didn't feel like her usual confident self.

Helping Velvet would in turn help her get that confidence back. Now was the perfect time. It would be nothing like the busy afternoon. Chelsie wouldn't be around to interfere. The indoor arena wasn't loud and crowded.

Now there was peace and quiet. Besides, desperate times called for desperate measures.

But if something went wrong . . . Ghostly images of getting injured or her dad being fired danced in her imagination. She blinked fast and replaced the images. She tried to imagine Velvet following Carolina's every direction as if the two of them were connected—like soul mates. Like in the video.

This hopeful goal spurred her determination. With the image of Tina Hodges and her horse in her mind, she grabbed the mare's lead rope and halter.

She carefully opened the stall latch and Velvet helped open the gate with her nose.

"You're impatient to get out, huh?" Carolina said, her voice shaky with nerves.

Velvet seemed to know they were doing something forbidden. Although she'd been anxious for the gate to open, once her halter was on, she hesitated.

"Come on, girl," Carolina coaxed her.

Trusting her, Velvet stepped over the entrance of what had been her home for the last few weeks.

Carolina opened the latch to the arena. Velvet waited patiently and then followed her in. Carolina hurried to close the gate, just in case. The last thing she needed was for the hot-blooded Thoroughbred to bolt out into the darkness of the night when the ground was frozen and slippery. Velvet could get seriously hurt if she got out to a strange place. If the mare escaped, there would be no catching her by herself.

Carolina took off the lead to let the mare become acquainted with her surroundings. Carolina was nervous, but she eased her breath.

Once she was free from the halter, Velvet sniffed the ground suspiciously. The footing was a mixture of sand and shredded car tires. Papi liked it better than plain sand because it minimized injuries to the horses, and the riders if they fell.

No. Not if. *When* they fell. The rider who hasn't fallen from a horse was a rider who didn't spend much time on one. Tina said that all the time.

But tonight, Carolina didn't expect to ride. She wasn't that foolish. This was for Velvet to connect with her.

Velvet eased her big body down to the ground with a groan and rolled, back and forth on her back, like a big puppy. Carolina smiled at her, glad that Velvet still remembered how to play.

Although her racing days were over, she was only five years

old, and hopefully had a lot of days ahead of her. Just imagining the amazing adventures the two of them could share together made Carolina's heart soar with hope and anticipation.

She couldn't wait to get to work.

She grabbed the long, straight whip that was hooked at the gate of the arena. But at the whistling sound of it in the air, Velvet scrambled to her feet.

She stared at Carolina like she'd been betrayed.

"I'd never hit you with it, sweetheart," she said in a soft voice, trying to smile so that Velvet would see she wasn't in any danger at all.

She would have to go through some desensitizing exercises so she wouldn't fear the whip, which was just a tool to help communicate, not a way to punish the horses. Carolina hadn't noticed when she watched Kimber and Velvet that the mare still wasn't used to it.

Velvet bolted and started running in circles so close to the wall, Carolina was afraid she'd hurt herself. This was nothing like the video sequence she'd memorized.

"Shhh," she shushed the mare, keeping the whip lowered to the ground and trying to control her own breath. Velvet didn't need to catch her fears and insecurities. The Thoroughbred already had enough of her own. Carolina felt the adrenaline coursing through the mare's veins like an electrical current. Electricity was good. It gave out light and warmth. But improperly directed, or in too high a quantity, it could cause a lot of damage.

She walked slightly behind Velvet as the mare galloped. Usually when doing groundwork, she'd start the horse walking, and then have it change directions. But now Velvet's eyes were showing a lot of white, and her ears were pulled back as if she were running from an invisible threat.

She was such an athletic creature that she could run and run without tiring, but soon, both girl and mare fell into a sort of trance. Velvet's step slowed into a canter and then a trot. Carolina lunged in front of her and, without missing a beat, indicated a change in direction. Velvet had no time to even think about rebelling and switched to trotting toward the left.

Like people, horses usually favored one direction over the other, and Velvet apparently had to concentrate more when trotting counterclockwise.

Carolina lunged in front of her again, and Velvet changed direction without hesitation.

"Good girl!"

Velvet seemed to sense the pride and happiness in Carolina's voice. She kept her ears and eyes alert toward her.

They were bonding!

She had done it. Carolina wanted to jump for joy.

Although she wasn't the one trotting and loping and the air was frigid, soon her armpits prickled with sweat underneath her many layers of clothing.

It was enough for one night.

"Whoa . . ." she said, and Velvet obeyed. She stopped trotting and snorted, a sure sign that she was relaxed.

This was the moment of truth, to see if they'd really formed a connection, an electrifying bond.

Carolina stood sideways and avoided looking Velvet directly in the eyes. She could only wait. A connection isn't something that can be rushed. Just like a friendship can't be forced because two people lived on the same ranch all of a sudden.

An owl hooted outside. Maybe it was the same one that

had seen Carolina sneak into the barn. Velvet's ears flickered. Carolina held her breath and tried to coax the mare with all the longing in her heart.

Finally, Velvet took a step in her direction.

"What are you doing?" A voice broke the moment like a shot in the mountains during deer-hunting season.

Carolina whipped around. On the other side of the arena gate, someone stood like an apparition.

Carolina screamed.

13

Whoa, Girl

"Why are you screaming?" the person hissed.

Carolina recognized the voice. Chelsie!

"You scared me!" Carolina whisper-shouted. "I thought you were a ghost or something."

"And I thought you were a thief!"

"A thief?" Carolina walked toward the edge of the arena. She didn't want to pass on her scattered emotions to Velvet. But it was hard to compose herself.

Chelsie had opened the gate and walked into the ring. "I came by to wish Velvet good night. Like every night for the last two weeks," she said. "What a surprise to see she wasn't there. No. I wasn't surprised. I was scared. And then angry. When I heard hoofbeats, I came out to see if maybe she'd escaped."

"How could she escape?" Carolina asked. "That's ridiculous!"

"She knows how to lift the latch when it's not locked. Aguasvivas is going to replace it."

Carolina's skin prickled. "You mean my dad?" She crossed her arms in a defiant gesture.

"I guess . . . yes, your dad," Chelsie said. "He said he'd do it today, and I wondered . . ."

"I'm sure he already did it. For your information, he's been working without a single day off for months! For years!" Carolina snapped. "And I'm not a thief! I was trying to help Velvet!"

"I don't need *your* help. Velvet and I were doing perfectly well," Chelsie said, her voice booming.

"It sure didn't look like it."

"Kimber and I have a plan, and you had to ruin it all with your nightly escapades. Now it's clear why Velvet didn't want to work with me. You've been stealing my place."

Carolina scoffed. She knew she should stop before she said something she'd later regret. But she didn't stop. "She doesn't want to ride with you because you're a stuck-up brat! You never cleaned a stall before coming here, did you?"

"You were eavesdropping on me and my mom that first day, weren't you?" Chelsie's hurt voice echoed around them.

"And you saw how mean Loretta and Tessa were the other day and didn't do anything to stop them!"

"You told them I worked at the barn like it was something to be embarrassed about!" Chelsie replied.

Velvet snorted in distress. Carolina turned away from the uncomfortable truth. Her temper got the best of her and made her tongue wag without filter, but now she had to focus back on the mare.

Right then, a breeze blew from the main barn entrance and the arena gate slammed shut.

Velvet neighed and spooked toward the girls.

"Velvet," Chelsie said as if she were trying to sound soothing, but her nervous voice wavered.

"Let me," Carolina said more forcefully than she meant to,

and raised her long whip instinctively as Velvet continued to feint toward them.

This was the wrong thing to do. Velvet startled hard at the sight of the whip; she cried out again and reared onto her powerful hind legs. Carolina gasped and backed away, but she stumbled and fell.

Chelsie reacted lightning fast.

She moved between horse and girl, her arms wide open as she kept her eyes on Velvet's. "Whoa, girl!" she said in a firm but soothing voice.

Velvet landed back on her front feet and studied Chelsie carefully. The fear and fight slowly leached out of Velvet as the three of them breathed in the cool night.

Carolina came out of her shock slowly. Her heart pumped so hard in her ears, it took a while for her to be able to hear the sounds of the night again. What could have happened flashed in front of her eyes. She could've been seriously hurt or even died! And it was her own fault—for arguing with Chelsie in front of the sensitive mare. And definitely her fault for raising the whip toward her.

The reality sank in. When Heather found out about this, her dad would lose his job. They would have to move. And Velvet . . . This might take her weeks or months to recover from. Forget about spring competition sign-ups! Velvet wouldn't be ready for a show for months. She would be sent off. Carolina would never see her again.

While Carolina was trying to sort through her fears, Chelsie had walked toward Velvet and clipped the lead to the halter, all the while murmuring into her ear things Carolina couldn't hear.

Carefully so as not to startle Velvet again, Carolina stood up, brushed the sand off herself, and walked toward Chelsie and Velvet.

Chelsie looked at her over her shoulder and asked, "Are you okay?"

Carolina was shaking. She pressed her lips so she wouldn't start crying. But she couldn't stop the emotions from rising inside her.

"Oh, Carolina," Chelsie said.

This might be the first time she'd called her by her name.

Carolina fell into Chelsie's arms and cried on her shoulder. "I'm sorry," she blubbered. She felt Chelsie stiffen—but then wrap an arm tentatively around her.

In an unexpected move that surprised both girls, the horse walked between them and curved herself around them as if she were trying to embrace both of them.

Without planning to, they encircled each other and Velvet with their arms.

"Thank you for saving my life," Carolina said.

Chelsie didn't say anything.

Velvet pawed at the ground, and Carolina said, "I'm sorry. I was thinking of myself instead of her. That's the worst thing I could have done." The words were easier to say with Velvet between them.

"Nobody got hurt."

"Thanks to you."

As quietly as possible, they made their way back to the stable, their previous argument forgotten, erased by both fear and gratitude.

Together, they brushed Velvet's coat and then cleaned her hooves. This time, their silence was soft and almost friendly.

They worked well as a team. Could they have been like this all along? So much wasted time!

Now it was too late. Chelsie was bound to tell her mom as soon as she went back to the mansion house. Carolina wanted to ask her not to, to keep this secret, but she didn't dare.

The clock on the barn wall marked two o'clock in the morning. There would be a lot of explaining to do the next day.

"I'm going to be a zombie tomorrow morning," Chelsie said.

Carolina thought she'd rather be a zombie than face the dire consequences her actions would bring.

Still, seeing the worry on Chelsie's face, she wanted to make it up to her in some way. "Don't worry. I can take care of it."

Chelsie's expression hardened. "You don't have to keep doing that."

"Doing what?"

"Trying to do it all. Just because we share chores doesn't mean I want to . . . I don't know, to take over the little barn, or the ranch, or even school, or something."

Chelsie had hit it on the head. When she said it out loud, it sounded silly to Carolina, even though that's exactly how she'd felt. Carolina realized she'd had things wrong the whole time.

"I'm sorry," she said again. "I know I've been . . . prickly. I want everyone to fit in here. Velvet. And me. And you."

Chelsie's face softened. She took a long breath, and Carolina thought the other girl would finally open up.

Instead, Chelsie sighed and kept rearranging the cleaning supplies, which already looked perfect.

Carolina turned around to hide her disappointment. After all, when she said she was sorry, she really meant it, even if Chelsie didn't accept her apology. Still, her heart hurt.

"Hey," Chelsie said in a soft voice, gently grabbing Carolina's arm.

Carolina turned around. The two girls were mirrors of each other's emotions, judging by their matching misty eyes.

"I'm sorry for what happened at school." Chelsie swallowed before she continued. "I was already upset my mom was too busy to drive me. You know? I was nervous about the first day of school. About fitting in."

Carolina almost laughed. "But you fit in better than me and I've lived here all my life."

Chelsie shrugged. "Loretta and Tessa have been nice to me, but they were mean to you. I should've said something. I'm sorry."

A warm feeling spread from Carolina's heart all the way to the tips of her long hair. She felt the warmth reach her eyes, and when she smiled, Chelsie smiled too.

"I'm sorry too," Carolina said. "I'm sorry for judging you without knowing what you were feeling."

How many times had her dad told her not to judge people by her expectations? Too many to count. Why hadn't Carolina been more accepting? Why had she let assumptions of who Chelsie was stand in the way of making friends with her before?

Velvet nickered and tossed her mane to the side, whipping both girls across their faces.

The girls smiled faintly. Carolina was scared for the morning. Judging by the paleness on Chelsie's face, the feeling was shared.

"I guess we need to head to bed," Chelsie said.

"I guess." They latched Velvet safely in her stall—they both double-checked the lock—and walked out of the large barn. Carolina took a deep breath and asked the question that stung her like a thorn. "Are you going to tell your mom?"

Chelsie swallowed and nodded. "I have to. I broke all the rules. It will break her heart."

Heat crept up Carolina's neck until she felt her whole head was on fire. "Actually, the one who broke all the rules was me."

Chelsie sighed. "Well, to be honest, you only beat me to it. I was planning on taking Velvet out to try some things I'd done in the past with other horses. I thought she'd pay more attention if there weren't so many distractions."

Carolina stumbled over her own feet. Those had been exactly her thoughts. She and Chelsie were on the same page after all.

Then Chelsie grimaced. "I don't have to tell her tonight though."

Gratitude washed over Carolina. "Maybe we can tell our parents together tomorrow morning."

Chelsie shrugged but said, "Maybe that's a good idea."

The darkness swallowed them both as they headed home. The truth was bound to come out with the sun tomorrow.

14

Pooper Scooping with a Friend

In the quiet of her room, Carolina lay back on her bed. She couldn't believe she'd been so reckless. So arrogant! What had she been thinking, taking Velvet out to the arena without asking for permission or help? And instead of letting Chelsie soothe Velvet, she'd insisted on doing it herself—and failed.

There were times when saying sorry definitely wouldn't cut it. This was one of those times. If she'd been up front with Kimber about the ideas she had for Velvet, then perhaps the trainer might have listened and tried to implement one or two things. Maybe she wouldn't have. But then Carolina wouldn't have put herself, Chelsie, and Velvet in danger.

How could she have thought that she alone had the secret to Velvet's recovery?

Kimber was an expert. What chance did Carolina have of better results all on her own?

None.

She'd been lucky that Chelsie had been there to save her. Carolina had to admit that even she made mistakes. What would have happened if Chelsie hadn't kept a cool head and intervened when she did?

And anyway, why had Carolina thought she was the only person who cared about Velvet? Chelsie visited her at night too. Chelsie wanted Velvet to succeed, even if she ended up having to move on. Because she truly loved the mare. Not just because she owned her.

Carolina slapped her forehead. She'd been so foolish!

Now she had to come clean about what she'd done.

The sky got clearer and clearer as her thoughts spiraled darker and darker.

It was pointless to go back to bed. She got dressed for the day.

A little while later, she heard her dad head out to the barn. From the window, she watched his lonesome figure as he trudged down the frozen lane. He stopped once to inspect something on the side of the path. He turned his hat backward.

What had he found?

He stood up and kept walking, hands pushed deep into his pockets. He looked worried, even from a distance.

The lights were on at the mansion and in the small stable. Chelsie must be there already.

The sound of the shower told her Mom was getting ready for her day too. Part of Carolina wanted to wait for her mom and tell her everything. She'd know what to do. How to fix the mess. But Carolina knew she had to speak with Chelsie first and then come clean to Ms. Whitby and accept the consequences for her actions.

With a heavy heart, she wrote a note.

At the stables helping Chelsie and then off to school!
See you later! I love you.
XOXO, Caro

She left it on the kitchen counter next to the coffee maker, which was already filling the house with the comforting scent of her mom's favorite drink. Mom would for sure see it there.

She had to fix her problems herself. It wasn't fair to throw this at her mom. Without another thought, she left for the barn.

There was a faint glow behind the mountains, and the frost crunched along with the gravel under her heavy footsteps.

As she got closer to the entrance, she was surprised to hear music playing. It was the type that Chelsie always had on. Carolina hadn't even asked what language the lyrics were in. The rhythm was energetic and catchy. It sounded like more than one boy was singing. In spite of her somber mood, by the time she stepped in, her spirits weren't so dark.

Chelsie was filling up the buckets with fresh water. Bella watched her with a contented expression on her face. It looked like she had found her next favorite human besides Tyler.

"Hey!" Carolina greeted her, grabbing a pitchfork to add hay to Pepino's feeder.

Chelsie didn't seem to hear, so she repeated louder, "Hey, Chelsie!"

Chelsie's head whipped toward Carolina and she screamed, "Ah!"

She dropped the bucket, splattering water all over the place. And herself.

Twinkletoes peeked his head out of his stall as if to assess the damage. Pepino lost no time and started eating hay.

"I'm sorry I scared you!" Carolina said. She rushed to grab a mop and start drying. The spilled water would freeze quickly and turn the barn aisle into an ice-skating rink. "I know. I must look like a zombie. I didn't sleep much."

Chelsie grabbed another mop, her thoughts obviously on the same wavelength as Carolina's.

She tried to smile but her eyes were droopy. "I'm sorry. It's not that you look scary! You just startled me."

"The music is kind of loud and you didn't hear me the first time," Carolina said.

Chelsie shrugged. "Sorry. The music helps me relax. And I think the horses like it too."

Carolina looked around and saw that they did. They were all relaxed in their stalls, waiting patiently for their food and their turn to be brushed and pampered.

The only ones that seemed anxious were the two girls.

That was the thing with horses. Although the past left marks on them, like the scar on Twinkletoes's ankle, they didn't obsess about their mistakes. And they for sure didn't stress about the future. They lived in the present. And right now? Right now, they were happy. They had a roof to protect them. Fresh hay to fill their bellies. Clean water. Plenty of love and care. They lacked for nothing.

But for all she loved horses, Carolina wasn't like them.

She had to face the mistakes she'd made the night before. And way before then. When she started judging Chelsie. For judging her for Loretta and Tessa's meanness.

The time to face the mistakes and start fixing them was now.

"Are you okay?" Carolina asked.

Chelsie shrugged, her lower lip a little quivery. "I'm just very—"

"Scared?" Carolina offered.

"I was going to say I'm just very sad."

Carolina paused, and hanging from the mop stick, she asked, "Why? Did anyone already find out? Did you tell your mom?"

Chelsie narrowed her eyes, confused. "No, I haven't yet. As far as I know, no one found out about last night. Besides, we said we'd tell them together, right?"

"Right," Carolina said, chided.

They kept working side by side, again in an uncomfortable silence. Carolina knew she had judged Chelsie only because she felt insecure about her place at the ranch. The knowledge didn't make her feel better.

Chelsie seemed lost in her thoughts as she freshened up the bedding. Suddenly, she asked, "So why exactly did you take Velvet out of her stall?"

Carolina stopped sweeping. She picked at the broom handle as she figured out how to express the whirlwind of her thoughts the night before.

"I've been watching videos on how to calm a skittish horse," she said finally. "It looked so easy on the screen." She didn't mention she thought she alone could help Velvet.

"But not at all in real life," Chelsie chimed in.

"Nope. Not in real life. I thought I'd learned this lesson when I tried to ride on an English saddle after watching a video," Carolina said with a groan. She was so embarrassed at the memory, she covered her face with her hand.

"You tried to ride English from watching one video?"

Carolina nodded, peering through her fingers.

Chelsie had her hands over her mouth, as if she was trying not to laugh. A snort escaped her.

Soon, they were both laughing.

As their giggles faded, Pepino sighed. His feeder was empty. He had a full tummy, at least for a couple of hours.

Carolina got a glimpse of the clock and said, "Ay! We need to hurry. I can't miss the bus, and we still have chores to finish before we talk to our parents!"

Chelsie grabbed another broom. "What are you waiting for, then?"

That spurred Carolina into action. For the next while, they worked in a frenzy. Chelsie seemed to have worked at the barn all her life. Whenever they could cut through the tension, they truly made a great team.

"So," Carolina said as she placed a little extra hay in Bella's feeder. "What's that music?"

Chelsie's cheeks were bright red, probably in a combination of cold and the exertion. "Oh, it's Velvet Lilly, this K-pop band."

"K-pop?" Carolina asked, intrigued.

She'd heard of K-pop before, but she didn't know much about it.

"Yes," Chelsie said, putting new hay in Leilani's stall, which had a net feeder instead of a trough like most of the others. She did it quickly and efficiently. "They're a brand-new band I saw in San Francisco last year."

"I've been to San Francisco!" Carolina said, placing Twinks's special feed in a bucket. "My parents are both from Los Angeles. I was actually born there."

Chelsie looked surprised.

"But we've lived here since I was a baby. This is the only home I've ever known." Sometimes Carolina forgot she was a California girl. People usually connected California to surfing and beaches, not horses. Here in Paradise, Idaho, she blended in. In most ways at least. "And how did you and your mom end up here?" Carolina asked.

Chelsie grunted as she lifted the net to the peg on the wall and said, "Hmm. It was a combination of things. When my great-aunt Bernice died, she left my mom, her only niece, all her money. Mom hated life in the city, and that's how she found this place to invest in."

So that was the famous Aunt Bernice!

"So you haven't been a horse girl all your life?"

Chelsie shrugged. "I started riding for real when I was nine, so two years ago. My dad is a horse trainer now, but he used to be a famous polo player."

Polo was not a sport Carolina was really familiar with. But if Chelsie's dad was famous, then she didn't want to offend her by saying so.

"What's his name?"

Chelsie sighed and hesitated before she said, "Milo Sánchez." She pretended to be busy with a strap from one of the feed buckets.

Carolina *had* heard of him! She'd watched plenty of his

training videos on YouTube. "Oh," Carolina could only say as her mind scrambled for words. "That's so impressive. Polo is like field hockey on horses."

Chelsie's mouth twitched in an almost smile. "Totally. So, my parents got divorced, and soon after my dad moved back to Argentina. He works on a team from Buenos Aires now." She said the city's name like someone who spoke Spanish. Carolina wondered if she did. "I guess when I was younger, I was so mad at him and my mom for spending all their time with horses that I just didn't want to step in the stables. Once it was just my mom and me, I had no choice. And what can I say? I love horses and riding. When I got into it more seriously, my mom and I started talking about everything. Not only horses. We became really close."

Carolina finished sweeping some of the grain she'd spilled on the floor.

"Do you see your dad much?"

Chelsie shook her head and her cheeks blushed. "Not really. Before the divorce he traveled a lot. Which caused all kinds of problems, I guess. And now . . . even with FaceTime and all that, it's hard to connect with him with the time difference. Maybe if I win a race or a competition, he'll care," she said. "Velvet looks like Paraná, a horse he had as a young boy. That's why . . ."

Carolina understood what Chelsie was trying to say. She felt lucky that Chelsie was telling her so much about her family.

Wasn't the love of horses a connection Carolina had with her dad and his side of the family too?

"All done," Chelsie said as she put the pitchfork on its hook on the wall. It was pretty straight.

"We're really done," Carolina said.

"I guess pooper scooping with a friend isn't so bad after all. Wait until I tell Loretta and Tessa."

They both smiled at the thought.

But Carolina's satisfaction faded when she remembered what came next. Now it was time to face Carolina's parents and Heather and tell them what had happened last night.

15

Nothing but the Truth

Carolina's stomach growled as she and Chelsie made the trek to the office in the big barn. The silence between them was charged with nerves. Carolina had been so anxious in the morning that she hadn't even considered pouring herself a bowl of cereal. But after the hard work in the little barn, she wasn't only nervous. Now she was also really hungry.

Breakfast would have to wait for later though.

"Good morning," JC said as he led the elegant gray Arabian to the pasture.

"Good morning," the girls replied.

They hadn't gone far when they had to get out of the way

so Andrew could walk past them. A beautiful sorrel quarter horse followed him meekly.

Carolina's hands itched with the urge to run her fingers through the luxurious manes of these new horses.

"Thank you! Good morning," Andrew said.

"Good morning," the girls replied in unison.

From the entrance to the wide aisle, they both looked down to Velvet's stall. Carolina saw a glimpse of her nose as she ate from the feeder attached to the half door, which meant she wasn't joining the rest of the herd in the pastures.

"Why is she staying in?" she asked.

Chelsie clicked her tongue and shook her head. "You saw how the other horses don't let her hang out with them."

The image of Velvet alone in the corner of the big pasture had been one of the reasons Carolina had acted so rashly the night before. She knew what Velvet must be going through. She remembered the long days of summer when Vida had been gone and she'd watched Tessa and Loretta ride together from afar and longed to be with them—or friends who loved horses as much as she did.

But hadn't she kind of done the same thing with Chelsie? Acted like the little barn was her little private club where Chelsie wasn't allowed? She regretted her actions so much now! Not only of the last night, but the last couple of weeks.

She followed Chelsie to the office. She was surprised to see both her parents, alongside Heather and Kimber, with somber faces all around. Papi's hat was turned backward, which was a sure sign he was worried about something.

They all smiled at the two girls, so Carolina assumed the long faces weren't due to Carolina and Chelsie. At least not yet.

Chelsie asked, "What happened?"

Heather pressed her lips together and pointed at the whip resting on her desk. Carolina's stomach dropped. It was the one she'd been using last night in her failed attempt to train Velvet—the one she had spooked Velvet with. What was it doing here?

"We found it in the indoor arena," Carolina's dad said. "I don't want to alarm you girls, but for the last couple of weeks, I've seen strange footprints outside the big barn."

"And instead of adapting, Velvet has been acting more anxious than usual," Kimber added. "It's not normal."

"Maybe someone has been lurking around the property?" Heather asked.

Carolina's mom sighed. "We've had stuff like this happen before. A couple of boys from town thought it was fun to play pranks when Mr. Parry would come visit. Silly things that had the potential to turn serious."

"Do you think that's it, then? Kids playing pranks?" Heather asked.

Carolina's dad shook his head, his face lined with worry. Maybe he was sifting through the entire boy population from town to find a suspect?

And the whole time the culprit was right in front of him. The staggering weight of her rashness made Carolina's shoulders hunch.

The conversation was definitely turning serious. The girls exchanged mortified looks. Chelsie's face had a greenish tint.

Before anyone jumped to wilder conclusions and Chelsie lost her breakfast or Carolina lost her nerve, Carolina said, "It's not boys from town."

The adults turned in her direction.

Her ears buzzed, but she still heard her mom's question. "How do you know?"

She wished she could turn back time and stop her past self from being so reckless. But that wasn't possible.

The only way out was through, which meant telling the truth.

"It was me," Carolina said. Her voice was muffled with tears. But she was determined not to cry. She stared at her shoes so she wouldn't see the disappointment in her parents' eyes.

It didn't help.

"'Me'? I mean, *you*?" Heather sounded as appalled as Carolina's parents looked.

Cheeks blazing with embarrassment, Carolina told them everything. How she'd been sneaking in to see Velvet. How she got the idea from the videos she liked to watch. And then, although it took a lot of courage, how she'd taken Velvet out of her stall and into the arena.

She kept her gaze on the ground as the whole truth unspooled from her lips, including the part in which Chelsie had come to her rescue or she might not be here telling the tale.

At the end of her confession, there was a ringing silence. Not a sound came from the stables either, as if even the horses wanted to hear what she was saying.

After reading the constant stream of books her mom brought from the library, Carolina had the impression that telling the truth would be like dropping a bundle of guilt off her shoulders. She'd always imagined this guilt as a heavy bag of horse feed. But it wasn't falling away from her. Instead, she felt the weight of her actions drop to her stomach.

She felt sick.

"Well," Carolina's dad said, his voice grave. "You're rash and impulsive, but I never expected this kind of behavior from you, Caro."

She looked up then. His eyes were blazing with a mixture of emotions she couldn't read.

"Thanks for helping Carolina, Chelsie," Carolina's mom said, her face pale and somber. "I don't even want to imagine what could have happened if you hadn't arrived at the right time."

Chelsie cleared her throat. "Actually," she said, and her voice was low but firm. "Carolina had everything under control before I got there. Then we started arguing, and Velvet got upset. The arena door slammed shut with the wind, and she spooked."

Carolina took a deep breath and added, "But you would have been able to calm her down if I hadn't insisted on doing it myself. I raised the whip off the ground and she *really* spooked."

"And what were you doing out of bed and in the arena last night?" Heather asked, her eyes boring into Chelsie.

Carolina wished she could say something that would get Chelsie off the hook, but she didn't know what.

Chelsie squared her shoulders and looked her mom directly in the eye. "I was just a few minutes late to do exactly the same thing Carolina was doing," she confessed.

"*Why?*" Now it was Kimber who spoke. "What were you girls thinking?"

Chelsie and Carolina looked fleetingly at each other and then away.

"I was scared we were running out of time," Carolina said.

"The sign-ups close soon," Chelsie added in a small voice.

"September seventh is next week." Carolina was surprised. Chelsie had been counting down too.

"What's this about the sign-ups?" Carolina's mom asked.

Again, Carolina took a deep breath and told the grown-ups what had been pinching her heart like a splinter. "Andrew and Kimber were talking about the sign-ups on the first day Velvet arrived. There were three weeks for Velvet to shape up before competition sign-ups. And if she can't get signed up now . . ." She twisted her fingers, still unsure what the rest of her sentence would be.

Chelsie nodded. "I thought Velvet would be re-homed if she didn't adapt. That day at the little barn when we were talking about Twinkletoes . . ."

"Exactly," Carolina added. For once, they agreed. "I thought that if she didn't improve enough for the spring shows, then she wouldn't have a chance."

The silence that followed throbbed.

"Well," Heather said, her voice a mixture of surprise and disappointment. "You two have weaved a story in your minds that has very little to do with reality. It's true Velvet isn't in a place to get signed up for the spring shows. But," she added, exchanging a look with Kimber, "that doesn't mean we're going to ship her away. Chelsie, maybe you can show on another horse." Chelsie opened her mouth to protest. "Or you can keep working with Velvet and wait until she's ready. I can tell you've really connected with her." Heather seemed proud about that. "But trying to take matters into your own hands was very irresponsible."

Carolina pressed her lips to stop their quivering so she could speak. She had to pay the consequences. But her parents didn't.

"Please, don't fire my dad and my mom. They have tried to teach me well. They love it here at Paradise," she said, gathering a lungful of air. "It's our home, and I promise this will never happen again. I'll . . ." Her mind tried to come up with a punishment strong enough to pay for her mistake. "I won't ride again until I've shown that I regret my decision. In exchange, I'll do anything you want me to do. But don't fire them, please?"

She blinked fast to prevent the tears from falling, but when she looked at Heather, she didn't see anger in her eyes.

"No one is getting fired," Heather said softly. She pressed

her lips before she continued, "I guess what you both need is a second chance. Paradise has always been a place for second chances, right, Amado?"

A second chance? Carolina couldn't believe her ears. But the grown-ups all seemed to know what was going on.

"You won't fire us?" Carolina asked.

Heather shook her head. "However, there have to be consequences for both of you girls."

Carolina sighed. She was so sorry for having dragged Chelsie into this mess.

An alarm chirped somewhere, and Heather looked at her smart watch.

"You should've been on your way to school a while ago," Carolina's mom said.

"Sorry I missed the bus," Carolina replied.

There was another pause.

"What if I drive these two to school and you parents think of a way they can make up for their mischief?" Kimber suggested. "I need to stop by Dr. Rooney's to get more ointment for Velvet's leg. The school is on the way."

All the parents exchanged a look, and then Carolina's mom nodded. "After school, come straight back home, Carolina. No stopping at the barn first. We'll need to talk."

"You too, Chels," Heather said.

And without another word, the two girls followed Kimber to her truck while their parents stayed muttering in the office.

16

Figuring Out the Social Vibes

Kimber's pickup truck was the coolest car Carolina had ridden in. It was navy blue with tinted windows. The wheels were so huge, she had to jump in order to climb into the cabin.

Unfortunately, she couldn't enjoy the ride to school. The endless expanse of country zipped by her window, but all she could see was the mistakes she'd made. Her stomach was still in knots after her confession.

Carolina was embarrassed for letting everyone down. Embarrassed that Kimber would think she was too impulsive and careless. Irresponsible.

Besides, what would Vida think when she saw her riding

with Chelsie to school? She wished she had a way to give her a heads-up.

"Don't be so hard on yourself, Caro," Kimber said, breaking the silence in the truck. She was looking at Carolina in the rearview mirror. "We all make mistakes. The important thing is to learn from them."

She sounded so forgiving and compassionate.

But could Carolina forgive herself? What had she learned last night? That trying to take over had only made things worse. That without Chelsie, it would have been even scarier. And that many times, she didn't have all the information to understand a situation. A couple of missing puzzle pieces could change the final picture.

She couldn't get a time machine to prevent last night from happening. But she could do something for the future, even if she couldn't do it alone.

"Thanks, Kimber," she said. "I know it was wrong to try to help Velvet all by myself. She has a full team of people wanting her to succeed. I don't know a lot, but I have some ideas. You all said she was anxious and getting bullied by the other horses, right? What about taking her to the small pasture instead of the big one with the other new horses?"

Chelsie turned away from the window. "Tell me more," she said.

Kimber looked at her in the rearview mirror.

Carolina got the courage to speak. "The other horses are used to being the center of attention. They're all young and spirited, and they're all trying to figure out their social vibes in a new place, you know what I mean?"

Chelsie nodded. "The horses from the small barn have all been here for a while. They feel stable and comfortable."

"They know they're loved," Kimber added.

"They have nothing to prove," said Carolina.

Now the silence in the car was electric with possibility.

"What Velvet needs the most is friends," Chelsie said. "Moving to a new place isn't easy. It's hard to figure out the— what did you call it, Carolina?"

"The social vibes," Kimber said.

Carolina's cheeks got hot again. She wondered if Chelsie

was talking about Velvet or herself. Maybe both.

By then, they'd arrived at the school.

The older kids all headed to their usual designated spots. Vida was talking to girls from their class.

Tessa and Loretta were waiting for Chelsie beside the flagpole. They waved at Kimber's truck with smiles from ear to ear. Carolina winced, thinking about what they would say once they realized she was riding along.

She and Chelsie exchanged a look. They had been doing so well. Was their relationship going to be one thing at school and something else at the ranch?

Carolina didn't want that. She wanted to apologize for what she'd told Loretta and Tessa in the cafeteria, about Chelsie cleaning the stables too. But the words were hard to say, so she chewed on them, stubbornly, like Pepino chewed on the grass that wasn't good for his tummy.

Kimber parked by the curb. Chelsie hesitated a little, as if she didn't know if she should wait for Carolina. But then she went ahead to meet Tessa, Loretta, and the rest of their group.

"That was a good idea you had. About Velvet, I mean," Kimber said. The truck revved when she switched it into gear. "I'll wait until you and Chelsie are back before I introduce Velvet to the little barn herd. Okay?"

"Thanks," Carolina said as she waved Kimber goodbye. That felt like a little spark of hope in her chest, but her doubtful voice still wondered . . . had her mistakes been so large that her dad wouldn't want her to help with the horses anymore? She'd have to make it through a whole day at school before she got to find out.

17

Second Chances All Around

Her teacher started the business of the day right away, and Carolina didn't have a chance to talk to Vida until the librarian came to pick up the class for library day. Today they would meet their reading buddies from the younger classes.

On the way to the media center, she and Vida could finally talk.

"Are you okay? I thought something had happened to you when you weren't on the bus," Vida said softly, her arms crossed as they walked side by side. Carolina didn't know where to start the story, and Vida said, "I'm glad you and Chelsie are friends."

She didn't put any special emphasis on the last word, but still, Carolina couldn't tell if her tone was jealous.

Carolina sighed. "Kind of friends." She looked over her shoulder. Chelsie and Loretta and Tessa were on the other side of the hallway talking among themselves. "Sorry I wasn't on the bus this morning."

Vida shrugged. It was time to bring her up to date on everything that had happened. In a rush, she started all the way at the beginning, with what had happened with Loretta and her brother the first day of school.

"Bracken?" Vida asked.

"The one and only."

"He *is* kind of a troublemaker. He and Cyrus play all the time."

"Cyrus was actually really nice about the whole thing. Unlike other people," Carolina said. She had to pause because the librarian, Mrs. Rouge, was starting to give directions. She didn't want to be called out. She wasn't the only one. The second graders stood next to the wall, quiet and big eyed.

Carolina felt a rush of tenderness looking at Cyrus,

Bracken, and the rest of their class. She remembered being in their exact same spot when she was their age. Her favorite reading buddy had been a girl named Molly Martin, who didn't mind reading the same horse books over and over with Carolina. She'd gone on to become their town's rodeo queen last Paradise Day Carnival.

"I'll pull out random names from this hat. You get who you get," Mrs. Rouge said, looking at the younger kids mainly. "And I'm sure at the end of the year you'll be good friends after bonding together with a book. Or many."

The little kids smiled nervously. Bracken Sullivan seemed to be avoiding looking at her. She averted her eyes. She didn't want to give him a hard time.

She didn't even have time to worry about who her buddy would be because the first names Mrs. Rouge pulled out from the sixth grade and second grade hats were "Carolina Aguasvivas and Bracken Sullivan."

Bracken's eyes went wide with surprise—and a little bit of fear.

Loretta had a guarded expression on her face as she stared

at Carolina, as if waiting to see her reaction, ready to jump to her brother's defense.

Time seemed to stop as Carolina realized there was a lesson here for her to learn.

Second chances.

Everyone deserved a second chance.

Papi,

Tyler,

Velvet,

Bracken,

Chelsie.

Some people, like Loretta, needed more than second chances.

Even Carolina needed second, third, and fourth chances! And she was grateful she might get that.

She made sure her smile for Bracken was inviting and sincere.

Vida pressed Carolina's hand in a gesture of support. "Good job," she whispered, and Carolina felt a balloon of light expand in her chest.

When Mrs. Rouge was done matching names, everyone stepped forward to pair up with their buddies.

"I'm sorry about the bottle," Bracken said as soon as he could. His shaggy blond hair stuck up in every direction. "I didn't mean to. It was an accident. It won't happen again."

What she'd done the night before had been a mistake more than an accident. She knew how he felt.

"I know," she said. "Now tell me, what do you like to read about?"

He bit his lip, and an adorable dimple flashed in his cheek. His blue eyes were bright with possibility. "Horses. You're the person who knows the most about horses in the whole school." He lowered his voice to a still-loud stage whisper. "Even my sister says that."

She closed her eyes and shook her head fast. Her ears weren't working.

"Your sister?" she asked in a surprised whisper. "Loretta?" Perhaps there was another sister she didn't know about.

Bracken scoffed. "Yep. Loretta. But don't tell her I told

you," he whispered back. "Now, can you help me find books about them?"

Carolina chuckled. "I'm not sure I know everything about horses, but I'll tell you all I know. Come on, the best ones are this way." She took him by the hand and led him to the few shelves that had books that he might like. There weren't a lot to choose from. But at least there were some great ones.

Bracken found the best reading spot, right next to Mrs. Rouge's fish tank. The tiny sea horse behind the coral seemed to get closer to hear Carolina's words.

She and Bracken sat side by side and she read aloud, "'The first place that I can well remember was a large pleasant meadow with a pond of clear water in it . . .'"

· ∪ ·

The fizzy feeling of having shared her love for horses with Bracken buoyed Carolina when the bell rang for lunch.

"I'll meet you at our table, Caro," Vida said. "I need to talk to my grandpa for a second."

Carolina gave her a thumbs-up and headed to the cafeteria.

To her surprise, Chelsie was at the entrance with Tessa and

Loretta. At the sight of them, the fizzy feeling left Carolina like a can of soda that had been open for too long.

But before she had time to turn around in the opposite direction, Loretta said, "Carolina," and stopped her in her tracks.

Carolina sighed. It seemed like today was a day for facing things she'd rather not. "If you're worried about—"

"I'm not worried about my brother, if that's what you're going to say," she interrupted her.

"You're not?"

"No. You were the top reader when we were little, so I know you'll help him okay. Besides, he's too adorable for anyone not to love him."

Carolina scratched her head. What was Loretta getting at?

Tessa tucked a strand of blond hair behind her ear. She seemed impatient too because she rolled her big brown eyes and said, "Stop going in circles! It's pizza day and all the Hawaiian will be gone first. You know it always is."

Behind them, Chelsie pressed her lips as if she was trying not to laugh. The more time Carolina spent with her, the more she realized what an interesting personality Chelsie had—once she warmed up to her surroundings.

Loretta took a long breath as if she needed extra courage. Carolina knew what that felt like too well. "I just wanted to say . . . I'm sorry for the way I reacted the other day with the bottle incident."

"And for calling me a pooper scooper?" Carolina said, a hand on her waist.

Loretta's cheeks went pink and she tossed her dark red braid over her shoulder. "Well . . . yes. Chels was telling me how you helped her learn her chores so she could ride Velvet, and that's cool."

Carolina sent Chelsie a grateful smile. "Sorry for being mean that first day in the cafeteria."

The words weren't that hard to say after all.

Chelsie shrugged and gave her a lopsided smile. "Everyone would know one way or another. If we all want to take lessons from Kimber, we'll all have to become pooper scoopers," she said in an amused voice.

Loretta blew like she was letting out steam from having to come to terms with this condition. "I know. Don't remind me."

"You snorted like a horse," Tessa said.

There was a small silence, and then they all burst into laughter.

Carolina wondered if those winds of change might affect more than she expected at the barn.

18

The Salt Block

In an unexpected turn of events, both of Carolina's parents were home when she arrived from school.

"But the chores, the accounting books," she mumbled in the middle of their kitchen, staring at them in shock.

"That can all wait, Caro," Papi said softly. "Mom and I want to know what has been going on in your mind lately."

"What drove you to an idea like that last night?" Mom added.

Carolina sighed and let her backpack fall to the floor, and she told them the truth. "I really don't know what came over me. I thought that I could help Velvet in secret, if it was just the two of us and quiet and peaceful. And then when she was well, I'd surprise you all and show you what a great team she and I made. Then everyone would see that I was still needed here. At the new ranch."

Papi scratched his head, as if the image Carolina's words painted made his skull itch.

"Ay, mi amor. Of course you're needed. And loved. At the end of all this, I hope that you learn an important lesson," he said.

Carolina thought for a second and then said, "That we must work hard for what we want?"

Mom made a hand gesture for her to continue.

"To stand up for what we believe in?" she tried again.

Her parents nodded, but she knew it wasn't the answer they were looking for.

She sighed, frustrated.

"That a single person can make a difference, but it does take a village, or a team, to change things for good," Papi said. "Just like it takes many hands to keep the ranch running, Velvet needs a lot of people to help her become the horse that she can be. Rest and structure are two things that will help her a lot."

"I guess we didn't really help with the structure," Carolina said. "And I think she needs friends too."

"You and Chelsie will be great for her," Mom said.

Carolina nodded. Now that she and Chelsie knew how to work together, she was sure they could help Velvet. But she was thinking of someone else. Many *someones*, in fact.

She told them the idea she and Chelsie had shared with Kimber in the car. About introducing her to the lesson ponies, the veterans of the old clinic.

Papi's eyes lit up. "That sounds like a great way to start. Let's see if it works!"

"And then we can talk about making up for that mischief, Caro," Mom said.

Carolina knew she wouldn't get off the hook. But now she was excited to see if her plan worked.

Papi texted Kimber, and a few minutes later, they all headed down to the small pasture.

Kimber, Heather, Chelsie, and Velvet arrived at the same time.

Carolina was still embarrassed to look Heather in the eye. By the color in Chelsie's cheeks, Carolina guessed she felt the same way. Velvet pawed at the ground as if telling everyone to get it together and stop making her nervous.

Little by little, Carolina was understanding that people, and animals, sometimes acted the way they did out of fear. All they wanted was love. Everyone deserved another chance— deserved not to be thrown away when they weren't helpful or when they made a mistake.

And she was grateful she had another chance to do better next time.

"Do you want to do the honors?" Heather said, nodding toward the gate to the ponies' pasture.

Carolina smiled and opened the gate.

Chelsie took the reins from Kimber's hands and led the mare in.

The ponies and horses, all standing calmly and munching on grass, looked up to see who was about to join them. Velvet nickered softly, tentatively. Her lips were tight. Her nostrils flared.

"You're going to love it here," Carolina whispered.

Velvet's head bobbed up and down as if she were saying

yes. Then she took off toward the far end of the pasture in a gallop that left a streak of color. Unbridled, she looked so happy. The other horses stopped chewing the year's last grass to see who was running by.

Pepino looked over his shoulder and stared at Velvet.

"Wow! She's so fast!" Carolina exclaimed, admiration in her voice.

Chelsie nodded. "She's like an arrow."

Like concerned mother hens, the girls watched as the horses started gathering around Velvet. Even from a distance, Carolina saw she still looked tense, ready to bolt again.

When Pepino headed toward Velvet, the mare neighed in warning, and unable to help herself, Carolina took a step in their direction. The memory of Velvet fighting with the other horses still haunted her. She didn't want Velvet hurting any of her friends.

"Wait!" Chelsie said, grabbing Carolina's arm.

Carolina's heart drummed, but she waited.

Velvet neighed again. The horses looked nervous—they milled around, everyone's ears swiveling to listen to each other. They had a system in place, a hierarchy, and they didn't know where this newcomer would fit yet. But the one who took the first step to bridge the gap was none other than the donkey, Twinkletoes.

In his characteristic old-man gait, he continued walking toward Velvet. He looked so determined, the mare seemed as stunned as Carolina, who'd never seen him take charge this way.

He and Velvet stood in front of each other, little gray nose to large black one. Plumes of steam rose in the air as they breathed into each other's nostrils. Carolina grabbed Chelsie's hand. This was a huge moment.

And then Velvet dipped her head and touched her nose to Twinkletoes's neck.

"Yes," Chelsie whispered.

A bubble of laughter rose in Carolina's throat, and she swallowed it. The last thing she wanted was to make a sudden noise and startle them and ruin this bonding.

The donkey and the Thoroughbred were just saying hi, but she had no doubt that they'd become fast friends.

Once they'd shared each other's breath, Twinkletoes turned around and walked away.

Velvet's stance looked way more relaxed now that she knew these horses weren't going to bully her.

And then Pepino and Leilani strode over to say hi to the newcomer. This time Velvet nickered and flicked her ears to the front of her head in a friendly gesture.

She touched noses with Pepino and Leilani too. After saying hi, they all retreated to their favorite corner of the pasture, where there was a huge block of salt for them to lick.

Velvet followed her new friends to the salt block, and they took turns licking. It was their hangout spot.

"Maybe things would be easier at school if there was a block of salt for the sixth graders to share," Carolina said.

"I think you might be right," Chelsie added.

The girls started laughing. But in the back of her mind, Carolina thought that horses were that block of salt for her. She'd become closer to Chelsie because of Velvet. She'd even made up—kind of—with Loretta and Tessa because of horses too.

"That's a lovely thing to see!" Kimber said. Carolina didn't know if she was talking about the horses or the girls. Maybe both. "You were right, Carolina! What Velvet needed was friends!"

Heather and Carolina's parents were talking among themselves. Carolina knew what came next, so she turned in their direction.

"Why don't we head back to our house?" Carolina's mom said.

Chelsie and Carolina shared a worried look. What kind of punishment had their parents agreed on?

19

Horse of My Heart

Carolina loved how cozy and inviting their cottage felt on this chilly autumn night. Mom brought over some apple muffins and tea, and they all sat around their kitchen table. Papi opened his laptop. A website under construction popped up on the screen. There was a bird's-eye-view photo of the ranch. If Carolina hadn't already been in love with this piece of pure horse country, she would've fallen head over heels right then.

Mom broke the expectant silence. "Heather, I think the girls are ready to hear about our plans. We'll need all their help to get this to work."

Heather nodded. "Considering their need to make up for last night, I think we'll find them a task."

Carolina and Chelsie exchanged another look. The girls couldn't stand the mystery anymore.

Finally, Heather said, "When Aunt Bernice passed away and left us a generous inheritance, I was thrilled that I'd be able to fulfill my lifelong dream of owning a horse property. When I was a little girl, I fell in love with Victory, the horse of my heart."

"Like Mr. Parry had Andromeda," Carolina said.

"My dad had Paraná," Chelsie said with a smile.

"And I had Capitán," Papi added, his eyes dreamy with memories. "But you don't really need one special horse to learn the lessons that changed my life."

Kimber nodded as if the words resonated with her. "I love working with horses I won't get to keep. That makes me happy."

Even though someday she'd love to have her own heart horse, like Kimber had Sadie, Carolina admired Kimber's attitude toward her job.

How lucky Carolina was to have grown up on a ranch and met so many wonderful horses. If only more people had this kind of opportunity!

"That's why when I found Mr. Parry's property was up for

sale, I called Amado and Jen," Heather continued, smiling at Carolina's parents. "We clicked straightaway. I can't bring my vision to life on my own, and they couldn't help this property without an active owner. We all have the dream to start the best horseback-riding school in the area. We need each other to make this dream come true."

"And we need you two to be on board," Papi said to Carolina and Chelsie. "In spite of the mistakes, I'm glad a shared love and concern for Velvet brought you together."

"We're hoping this place will soon be ringing with the voices of young people learning to love horses and all the things they can teach," Heather said. "Talking around town, I found there is a lot of interest in the place we want to build."

"Not everyone will be able to pay though," Carolina said, thinking of how the riding clinic had failed before. Also, about how even though her parents worked at the ranch, she still had to learn on her own because formal lessons were so pricey.

"That's a very good point, Caro." Her mom nodded at her.

"True," Heather agreed. "We'll need a few more lesson horses, and of course Kimber is here to help. I want this place to be special. To stand out from what the other riding schools offer."

There was a brief silence in which they were all thinking.

"Mom, you said you wanted people to learn every aspect of taking care of the horses," Chelsie said, speaking for the first time. "What if there's an extra incentive for those who volunteer at the barn to earn riding time?" A tiny smile lit up her face.

"You mean including scooping poop, and other tasks?" Carolina asked.

Chelsie nodded. "And for the younger kids who can't do a lot of the work, what if they volunteered to read to the horses? It would be a win-win situation."

"Reading buddies!" Carolina exclaimed.

Carolina's mom nodded. "Recently at the library, we've had a dog that comes over every other Friday to help emergent readers. The program is a huge success! Kids' reading skills grow so much when they read to an animal."

"And the animals of course love it," Papi said.

"We can do something similar," Carolina said, the image of Bracken popping into her mind.

"But how do we make everything work? Even with volunteers, horses and food and trainers cost money," Mom said. Numbers were always in her mind. She was the ranch's account keeper, after all.

The kitchen was electric with the energy of three parents, a trainer, and two girls trying to find a solution.

Soon, enthusiastic ideas started flowing. Heather jotted them down with a smile on her face:

Riding skills

Read to a horse

Confidence

Trust

Dreams

Mentoring

Scholarship

Paying it forward

Soon, she had a long list. She looked at it for a second and then looked up at the two girls. Carolina sat at the edge of her seat, wondering how she could help make all these fantastic words a reality.

"Like Amado said, you two make a great team," Heather said. "What if you girls come up with a plan to include our whole community in our dream?"

Carolina was surprised. But if Heather was asking her to contribute to this new adventure, then that had to mean she considered her an indispensable part of the Paradise team.

Besides, she and Chelsie had reached a good rhythm at the barn with chores. They were getting along even though they were so different from each other. They were two sides of the same coin, and that's why they would work well together.

Apparently, the same thoughts were going through Chelsie's head. She and Carolina exchanged a look and they nodded.

"Let's get to work, Aguasvivas," Chelsie said. "What do you think?"

· U ·

For the rest of the evening, the two girls worked in the cottage kitchen, making a presentation for their parents. Right after chores, their parents and Kimber gathered again to see what they had come up with.

They took turns sharing the plan they'd drawn on poster board: Paradise Ranch would host a riding school. Every student would have to volunteer to clean stalls and groom horses, or read to them, as part of the program. They could earn extra lessons with this work.

Before Carolina announced the best part, she looked at Chelsie for approval.

Chelsie nodded, and Carolina continued, "We'll also have a mentoring program. Riders with more experience will show the ropes to the new ones. Besides riding horses, the funnest thing in life is sharing that love and knowledge with others." Carolina used her best school presentation voice, feeling official. "Our favorite part is that Chelsie and I hope we can establish a scholarship for one student every three months or so, to make the lessons available to those without the financial means. We can match students to different horses so they get to experience the joy of bonding with a horse."

Kimber was the first one to clap. Carolina felt a warmth spreading in her chest seeing the look of pride and satisfaction on her parents' faces.

"I love Paradise with all my heart," she said, fighting not to cry with emotion. "And when you love something, you share it with everyone instead of keeping it all for yourself, right?"

"Right," her dad said.

"I love this," Heather said. "We'll need to figure out how to cover the sponsorship. I'm sure we can do something. I've done fundraising before."

Chelsie spoke up. "Carolina and I thought maybe the community would step in to help. Like neighbors helping neighbors," she said, seeming a little less nervous to share with Carolina nodding at her side.

"What a great idea, you two," Heather said. Her eyes shiny with enthusiasm, she added, "Now, a name. Have you thought of one yet?"

Carolina was ready. The name had come to her as if a muse had whispered it in her ear. "What about Unbridled Dreams?

Remember how Velvet ran across the paddock, unbridled, as if she were running to her dreams? Didn't you all want to be like her for a second?"

"I love it," Carolina's mom said as Heather jotted it down in her notebook.

"We'll be ready to take our first students for the riding school by the end of October," Papi said. "What do you think if we start taking applications for the scholarship now and inaugurate it all in December? That way, our students who wish to can sign up for the summer shows." He sent Chelsie a pointed look.

Her cheeks were tinged pink when she nodded.

Carolina felt a twinge of jealousy at first, but then she waved the feeling away. She really had no interest in the shows. Her biggest desire was to help Velvet achieve her potential, even if it was with a rider who wasn't her.

"That'll give us the chance to sponsor three students before the big Paradise parade at the end of summer," Carolina's dad said.

Carolina already saw herself heading the Paradise delega-
tion, but then thought better of it and replaced the mental
image with her and Chelsie riding side by side.

"A year is a great time frame to see if the system is working," Mom said, and Heather agreed.

They spent the next hour dividing up their tasks over
pizza—the frozen kind because no one would deliver to the
ranch.

Kimber, who'd majored in horse therapy in college, would be
the head of the program and train new instructors. Carolina's
mom would make sure the numbers were balanced and made
sense. Papi would be in charge of teaching how to take care of the
horses. Heather would gather sponsors to cover the scholarships.

"And what will Chelsie and I do?" Carolina said.

"You will get all your friends interested in joining us at
Unbridled Dreams. And for now, you can start mucking up
the little stable and bedding the horses. Prepare the big stall
for Velvet," Papi said.

"And next week, after your grounding is over, we can start

keeping track of your work hours so you can earn your riding lessons. What do you think, Carolina?" Heather said.

Chelsie winked at her. Carolina smiled.

Being grounded at the barn with a friend didn't seem like a grounding at all.

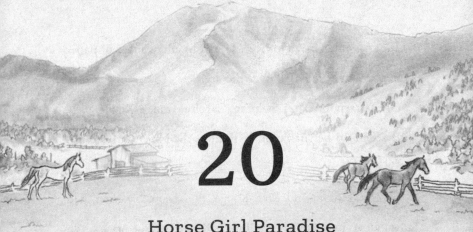

20

Horse Girl Paradise

The next few weeks went by in a whirlwind of change as the ranch prepared for the winter months and starting the new Unbridled Dreams program. Carolina and Chelsie became the program's ambassadors at school. When Loretta found out she could earn extra lessons with every hour she volunteered to muck the stalls, she smiled cunningly.

She was so competitive, the idea of earning more than anyone else made her excited.

Things are going to get very interesting at the barn with so many big personalities, Carolina thought.

Every day, the list of prospective students grew. Papi kept it by the computer in the office. He had to add a sheet of paper to fit the names from all over the area.

One afternoon after helping Carolina muck Bella's stall, Vida scribbled her name on it, right at the bottom of the list, but it was there.

Carolina's mom and Mrs. Rouge, the school librarian, had joined forces for a holiday reading challenge, and the prize was a weekend at the barn. Last time Carolina checked the standings, Bracken Sullivan had read the most out of all the second graders.

She couldn't keep up with his voracious reading, so she was always on the lookout for new books for him. They'd moved on to nonfiction and soon, he'd declared his favorite horses were Thoroughbreds. He and Velvet would get along grandly.

· U ·

The last Saturday in November, Carolina was getting ready to head down to the barn for her chores. She was trying to get the scarf Vida had gifted her around her neck when her mom stopped her.

"Let me help you," Mom said, helping her tuck the ends inside her jacket.

Carolina rolled her eyes, but she was grateful that her mom was looking out for her. She didn't want to get sick the week before Unbridled Dreams officially opened.

"And what's that?" she asked, pointing at a package wrapped in colorful paper on the table.

"Oh," Mom said with a wide smile. "It's for you and Chelsie. But don't open it until you're in the barn. Now go, I saw Chelsie already heading there."

"Thanks, Mom," Carolina said, and kissed her mom on the cheek. "See you later."

She opened the door and took a lungful of crisp mountain air.

A horse nickered in the distance, and the sun was starting to peek out from behind the White Cloud Mountains.

She broke into a run and headed to the stable.

The scent of musky horses and sweet hay was the best mood lifter ever.

"Good morning, my loves!" Carolina said.

Five heads looked over their stall doors to say hi. Velvet was in the last one across from her best buddy, Twinkletoes, and seemed to smile at her. The mare had been doing so much better as she bonded with the old lesson ponies. Her leg was healed, and her spirit was healing too. Though the date for spring sign-ups had sped by them all without fanfare, Velvet would definitely be ready for summer shows. Kimber and the girls had been deliberate and structured with their training, and Kimber had been able to ride the mare consistently. Carolina was so proud of the work she'd *helped* accomplish.

"Good morning, sleepyhead," Chelsie said, coming out from Pepino's stall with a rake full of manure to put in the wheelbarrow.

"Good morning," Carolina replied. "Here. This is for us."

Chelsie smiled. She loved getting presents. Together, they ripped the wrapping paper.

"T-shirts?" Carolina said.

"Matching T-shirts," Chelsie exclaimed.

They each held an orange shirt and read in unison, "Unbridled Dreams."

"Look on the back!" Carolina said, turning the shirt over for Chelsie to see. It was a line drawing her dad had done of Velvet and Twinkletoes. Above their faces was the phrase *Welcome to Paradise*.

"It's perfect!" Carolina exclaimed, putting on the T-shirt over her sweatshirt. Chelsie followed suit.

Carolina was about to grab a broom to start her chores when Kimber opened the door. She wore a sky-blue version of the shirt. "Good morning! I'm glad to see you both here. I love the new shirts!"

"Good morning," the girls replied.

"Are you helping us with chores?" Carolina asked with a mischievous smirk.

"Actually, I have a surprise for both of you," Kimber said. "Carolina, bring Velvet, please."

Carolina obeyed without question and grabbed the lead rope, then led Velvet out to the arena where Kimber and Chelsie were heading.

The gray Arabian horse, Shadow, was already saddled up.

There, beside the gate, was a saddle stand with Velvet's tack.

"Get her ready, please," Kimber said, and again, Carolina obeyed. As Chelsie held Velvet's lead rope, Carolina carefully followed the steps of tacking up the horse. And when she was done, Kimber said, "Caro, why don't you bring the mounting block and get on Velvet? Chelsie, Shadow's ready."

Carolina couldn't believe her ears. "What?" she asked, emotion making her eyes cloudy.

Chelsie nodded. "I want to start practicing for next year's jumping competitions, so Kimber suggested I ride Shadow more. We want your help with Velvet. She needs a calming voice and a soothing touch. And that's you. She has to be ready for our first batch of students next month."

Without waiting to be told twice, Carolina got in the saddle.

Velvet waited patiently.

Their dreams were unbridled, but for now, they walked together into the indoor arena.

Acknowledgments

This book wouldn't have been possible without the brilliant guidance and feedback of my dear editor, Olivia Valcarce. I'm so honored I get to collaborate with you on a story that would have meant so much to the little girls we once were!

It takes a village to create books and bring them to readers' hands. Thank you to the whole team at Scholastic, including Aimee Friedman, Stephanie Yang, Winona Nelson, Caroline Flanagan, Mary Kate Garmire, Elisabeth Ferrari, Rachel Feld, and Jordin Streeter. To the Book Clubs and Book Fairs teams, thank you!

All my gratitude to my agent, Linda Camacho, and the Gallt & Zacker Literary Agency.

Cindy Powell, thank you for being a wonderful riding instructor! To the team at Bridle Up Hope, I admire you all so much! Thank you for the amazing work you do helping girls and women find confidence and resourcefulness while connecting to horses. Your motto "Changing lives. One girl and horse at a time" changed my life and inspired me to help others!

Natalie Mickelson, Rachel Seegmiller, Verónica Muñoz, and Carmen Rodriguez Hernandez, thank you!

Thank you to all the librarians, teachers, mentors, and parents for your support. Thank you, readers, for reading my stories and loving my characters.

And last, but never least, gracias a mi familia, los Saied y los Méndez, especialmente Jeff, Julián, Magalí, Joaquín, Areli, Valentino, Nova, Cora, y Rosi. ¡Los quiero!

Dear Reader,

Welcome to Paradise Ranch!

Growing up in Rosario, Argentina, I wasn't able to ride horses much myself. So instead, I read books about horses over and over until my copies fell apart. They helped me experience the magic of horses until I was lucky and privileged enough to ride when I got older. Horses have taught me a lot, and just like Carolina, when I love something, I want to share it with others. Whether or not you get to spend time with horses in real life, I hope that the kids and horses in this series become your lifelong friends.

If you want to learn more about horses, here are just a few websites that have advice—from taking care of horses to finding chances to volunteer with them. Check them out with your guardian's permission:

Horse Rookie: horserookie.com

An educational website dedicated to helping equestrians of all levels (especially newbies) gain knowledge and have fun! They're also committed to highlighting diversity in the horse-riding community.

Bridle Up Hope: bridleuphope.org

Changing lives. One girl and horse at a time.

American Hippotherapy Association: americanhippotherapyassociation.org

Thank you for reading! See you on the range!

Yamile

Yamile Saied Méndez
Alpine, Utah

Here's a sneak peek at
Horse Country #2: Friends Like These!

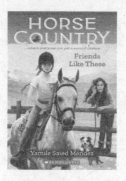

"While they talk here, do you want to come see the little barn with us? You can meet the lesson horses and get some hands-on experience," Chelsie said.

Gisella looked panicked, clutching her welcome gift bag, which she hadn't opened yet. She hadn't even peeked inside.

"I'm okay staying here, actually." Gisella stepped closer to her dad.

Her jaw was set in a stubborn gesture that reminded Carolina of Twinkletoes when he refused to eat his special feed. But every time Gisella made eye contact with her parents or Kimber, she smiled, as if she were the happiest girl in the world.

What kind of sorrow did this girl hide behind her pretty smile?

Once they had gone over the paperwork, Mr. Bassi said to

Gisella in Spanish, "I'll come get you in an hour's time." This time, he spoke slowly enough for Caro to understand.

Gisella turned toward him with urgency. This time there was no smile on her face. "Can you just wait for me here?" she asked in Spanish.

Kimber nodded and, looking at Gisella's parents, said, "Of course, you're welcome to wait for her."

Turning to Gisella, she added, "During the first lesson, Carolina and Chelsie will introduce you to the lesson horses and show you how to take care of them. Then we can go on a little turn around the arena."

Gisella grabbed her mom's hand. "I don't want to ride a horse yet. I'm scared."

Carolina had not expected this.

The first student they were sponsoring was terrified of horses?

Had there been a misunderstanding somewhere?

Kimber and Chelsie didn't seem to appreciate the seriousness of this fact. If Gisella didn't even want to be here, then what kind of feedback letter would she write to the donor? What if she wrote a bad review and then they had to close Unbridled Dreams?

More adventures await
you at Paradise Ranch!

Keep an eye out for more books
in the Horse Country series!

·U·